SAVING IMOGENE (SPECIAL FORCES: OPERATION ALPHA)

SEAL TEAM TANGO, BOOK 1

NICOLE FLOCKTON

D1257138

Dear Readers,

Welcome to the Special Forces: Operation Alpha Fan-Fiction world!

If you are new to this amazing world, in a nutshell the author wrote a story using one or more of my characters in it. Sometimes that character has a major role in the story, and other times they are only mentioned briefly. This is perfectly legal and allowable because they are going through Aces Press to publish the story.

This book is entirely the work of the author who wrote it. While I might have assisted with brainstorming and other ideas about which of my characters to use, I didn't have any part in the process or writing or editing the story.

I'm proud and excited that so many authors loved my characters enough that they wanted to write them into their own story. Thank you for supporting them, and me!

READ ON!
   Xoxo
   Susan Stoker

To Christine and Rebecca thanks for being wonderful fans and Ninjas

CHAPTER 1

NAVY SEAL LEIGHTON "BIRD" NELDER LOOKED OVER THE gathering and wondered why the hell he'd let his brother talk him into coming. Parker, or "Spider," as he was known to his crew, had convinced him the firefighter fundraiser was just what Bird needed. The second he'd arrived, he knew his brother had been way off the mark.

Most of the people attending were families. Couples. People in love. He spied one such couple on a picnic bench, kissing as if they couldn't get enough of each other and their reason for living was the other person.

He sighed. He'd had that once. A lifetime ago. Then he'd messed it up and let it go.

His fingers went to the chain around his neck and, lifting it from beneath his shirt, he touched the wedding band that had adorned his finger for five years. Happy years, he'd thought, but apparently, he'd been wrong. His career was hard on his loved ones and Imogene had struggled. Understandable, given her past, and he'd tried to reassure her that he wasn't her parents, but it hadn't been enough. When he'd come back from a mission, he'd found her gone. All she'd left behind was a note saying she was sorry and she would be in touch. It had gutted him.

That had been almost two years ago and he still hadn't searched for her. And she hadn't searched for him. In the eyes of the law, they were still married. Parker was continually on him to find her and get a divorce so that he could move on. But Bird always found a reason not to.

Even after all this time and her betrayal, he still loved her. Every time he saw a dark-haired woman about the same height as Imogene, his heart skittered, thinking he'd found her. But he was wrong. It was never his wife.

Swallowing the last of his water, he pushed away from the tree he'd been leaning against and made his way toward one of the trash cans. Before he could reach it, a toddler came barreling into his legs. On reflex, with one arm, he grabbed the little girl so she wouldn't fall on her bottom.

The empty bottle slipped from his fingers as he looked into the child's face. Her eyes were a piercing green the exact same shade he saw every day when he looked into the mirror. On her chin was a little indentation that matched his own.

Was this little girl his?

It can't be. And where the hell did that thought come from?

"Layla, don't run off like…"

Bird looked up and stared into the eyes of the woman he hadn't seen in almost two years. His wife and, apparently, the mother of his child.

"What the fu—?" He swallowed down the curse.

"Leighton." Imogene's face paled. She scooped up the little girl, holding her close to her chest.

His fingers itched to reach out and touch the blond curls on the baby's head. She had to be his. There were too many familiar features on her face that matched his own. Not to mention the way Imogene looked like she was about to pass out.

Words bubbled up inside of him, but his brain refused to engage and blurt them out. This had to be a dream. He'd wake up in the crappy apartment he now lived in, in Riverton, California. Not the house they'd purchased. The house they still owned, but he had rented it out because he hadn't been able to bear the thought of selling it. Bird closed his eyes and counted to five before opening them.

Everything was as it had been a few seconds ago. "Imogene, what's go—?"

"I'm sorry," she whispered before turning and hurrying away from him.

It took a second for him to comprehend what was happening and then he was off after her. No way was he letting her disappear again. Not when he had so many questions that needed to be asked.

In three strides he'd caught up to his wife and was walking beside her. His fingers itched to reach out and touch her, to trace the familiar curve of her elbow. The shape of her face. The gentle sweep of her eyelashes fluttering down when he came in to kiss her.

They may have been apart for two years, but he hadn't forgotten a thing about her. She was his wife. And that annoyed the shit out of him. Underneath all the anger steaming through him at all she'd kept from him, his reaction at seeing her again was the same that had swept over him when he first saw her—need and desire.

"Stop, Imogene. We need to talk."

3

"We've got nothing to talk about, Leighton."

He snorted. "Nothing to talk about. That's rich, considering we appear to have had a child together. A child I know nothing about." He kept his voice low as he didn't want to make a scene, but it was getting harder and harder to contain his anger. Not that he'd ever hurt Imogene or her daughter. He'd sooner stab himself with his own Ka-Bar than lay a finger on either of them.

Imogene stopped abruptly and he had to backtrack a couple of paces. When he faced her, his anger faded and despair replaced it. The haunted look in his wife's eyes was one he'd never seen before. He raised his hand to brush his knuckles down her cheek, a gesture he'd always done with her, but he dropped it when she flinched back.

"I'm sorry, I shouldn't have said we had nothing to talk about. You're right, we have a lot, but I can't do this right now, Leighton. Please. It's not the place." Her lips compressed and she squeezed the child, burying her face in the sweet blond curls before looking back at him. "I can't believe you're here. How did you find me?"

"Dumb-ass luck. Parker's a firefighter here in San Antonio and he dragged me along. I had a couple of days off and he invited me out to visit him. I hadn't seen him for a while so I took him up on his offer. The last person I expected to see here was you." He shook his head, still not believing he was talking to his wife.

They stood there looking at each other. He didn't know what else to say.

When his text messages, calls and emails had gone unanswered, and all her social media accounts had been closed, Bird had accepted that Imogene didn't want to be found.

Nor did she want anything to do with him. Now he knew why. She wanted to keep his child from him, but even that didn't make sense. Imogene wasn't a vindictive person and they hadn't had a fight before he'd gone on that mission. The mission that was supposed to have been straightforward, but had ended up going to shit. They'd been caught in the middle of an uprising and had been unable to be extracted for six weeks. In the end, he'd been gone two months.

"I, um, I…" she glanced over her shoulder at the crowd of people. No one was paying them any attention but she had to have come with someone. Had she moved on? Was she seeing someone else?

The thought of dating another woman had been abhorrent to him. When he'd spoken his wedding vows, he'd meant them. He'd had the means to find out where she was. One phone call to Tex, the former SEAL who worked with all arms of the military using his computer skills in ways Bird couldn't even fathom, and he would've had his answer. But he hadn't want to accept that his marriage was over. Hadn't want to accept that he'd failed his wife. That he hadn't seen the signs that she was unhappy. So he hadn't placed that call.

"Answer me one thing, Immy, please." Her nickname slipped off his tongue as though it hadn't been years since he'd uttered it.

Her eyes widened again and her face seemed to go even paler. Did he really have to ask her? She had to know what he was about to say to her. She bent and kissed the top of the child's head. "Yes," she whispered. "Layla is your daughter."

He clenched his fists and pressed them hard into his

5

eyes, to crush the unexpected rush of moisture from spilling over.

He had a daughter.

* * *

THE LOOK of sheer delight on Leighton's face pummeled Imogene's belly, like Layla had seemed to enjoy doing inside of her while she'd been pregnant with her.

Her husband had been the last person she'd expected to see when she accepted her neighbor, Brent's, invitation to come to this picnic. She hadn't seen the harm in going, even though Brent's interest in her seemed to be going from friendly neighbor to a man wanting more. Something she wasn't ready to give.

She'd long ago accepted that Leighton had made his decision, and that he didn't want anything to do with her or their child. But seeing the rush of emotions crossing his face when she'd confirmed his suspicious, belied his actions.

Confusion swept up inside of her. They needed to talk. But voicing her thoughts and fears had always been difficult. Avoiding conflict had been the way she'd gotten through a horrible childhood, where her parents constantly fought, and if she said something or smiled in a certain way, both of them had thought she was trying to pick a fight with them. In the end, she'd kept her mouth shut and, the day after high school graduation, she'd taken the first bus out of Root Flats, Nevada. Not caring where it was going, she'd just wanted to escape.

She'd landed in Riverton, California. The sun and beach had been what she'd needed to start over.

"We need to talk, Imogene." Leighton's whiskey-smooth voice brought her back to San Antonio.

A sigh shuddered through her. "I know."

Layla chose that moment to wriggle her small body. "Down," she demanded. At not quite two, she was already displaying a determination to do her own thing and her favorite words were *up, no,* and *down.*

Reluctance to let her precious baby out of her arms swirled through her, but the last thing she wanted was for Layla to throw one of her almighty tantrums. The terrible twos were approaching and it was a phase she wasn't looking forward to going through alone.

You don't have to now, do you?

She shushed that inner voice, but placed her baby on the ground. Layla took a couple of seconds to steady herself before she toddled over to Leighton. Imogene clasped her hands together to stop herself from snatching her child back into the safety of her own arms.

Even though she'd walked out on her husband, it hadn't been his fault. Not really. Besides, there was no way he would hurt his daughter. He was a Navy SEAL, and their job was to protect and save. Hurting a toddler wasn't in his wheelhouse.

Holding her breath, she watched as her daughter stopped in front of her father. Layla then grabbed his jeans. "Up," she demanded.

Imogene's eyes flew to Leighton's, gauging his reaction at his daughter's demand. His green eyes darkened, reminding her of how they'd always looked before he'd entered her body. Only now, there was a slight sheen to them, as if he was holding back tears. Shock slammed into her and her heart clenched. Navy SEALs weren't ones to

7

show their emotions. But then again, he was meeting his daughter for the first time.

Would he have looked like this the first time he'd seen the ultrasound photo of her? Or the first time she kicked? Or when he held his daughter for the first time, moments after her birth?

Unequivocally, yes. She had no doubt her husband would've shown his daughter the emotions he seemed to fail to show her.

"Is it okay?" he asked and a tiny crack formed in the concrete casing she'd erected around her heart when she'd made the decision to walk away.

She nodded, words impossible.

He hoisted Layla up and the little girl giggled in delight. She held up her chubby arms. "Up."

Leighton chuckled and a million memories of the two of them laughing together played in her mind. All it had taken was one look from him and the floodgates she'd tried so hard to keep barricaded shut, opened and spilled into her.

"You can't go much higher than what you already are, princess."

"Up," the little girl repeated.

"I'd listen if I were you. She's pretty determined, even at eighteen months." Imogene had plenty of experience at how high Layla liked to go. She wasn't as tall as Leighton, so her daughter was delighted when he lifted her a little higher. Her giggles started up again and when Leighton pulled her close to his chest, she rested her tiny head on his shoulder and sighed, as if she'd done it a hundred times and wasn't meeting her father for the first time.

"Jesus Christ, Imogene, why?" She could tell he wanted

to say more, but he was keeping his emotions in check so as not to frighten their daughter. For that, she was grateful.

How could she explain? So many circumstances had conspired against her that, in the end it became easier to start over. She'd meant to...she'd tried...but she'd been wrong all along, a fact that had hung over her all this time.

"Hi, Layla, I'm your daddy." The whispered words were a knife to her heart. She couldn't look at him because, if she did, she was going to break down, and for the last two years, she'd managed to keep her emotions about Leighton and their marriage in check.

"Hey bro, where did you get the kid from?"

Imogene cringed inside when she recognized Parker's voice. She hadn't seen him since the Thanksgiving before she'd walked out on Leighton. It had been the first family Thanksgiving they'd been able to host where Leighton wasn't away on a mission. The day had been amazing and the night even better.

The one place they'd always connected had been the bedroom, but it wasn't enough in the end.

Leighton moved to her side and juggled Layla so that he was able to sling an arm around her shoulder. The heavy weight was familiar and it was as if the past two years of separation hadn't happened. He turned them so they were facing his brother. "Parker, I'd like you to meet my daughter, Layla."

Imogene would've laughed at the way Parker's mouth dropped open if she hadn't heard the death knell sounding on the life she'd known for the past two years.

There was no going back now.

CHAPTER 2

"WHAT THE FUCK, BRO?"

"Language, Parker." Bird immediately covered his daughter's ear that wasn't pressed against his chest. At least he'd swallowed the curse when he first saw Layla. He couldn't believe he was holding his daughter in his arms and she didn't seem afraid of him either. As if she instinctively knew that he wouldn't harm a hair on her head. And he wouldn't. Now that he was aware of her existence, he wasn't going to let her out of his life.

"Sorry. I don't understand any of this. How do you know she's not lying? You haven't seen *your wife* in two years," Parker demanded, as his lips firmed into a thin line.

"I'll show you." He hefted his daughter higher in his arms. "Layla, sweetheart, say hello to your Uncle Parker. Parker, I'd like you to meet your niece, Layla."

God, saying the words out loud still didn't feel real. Somehow, anger at Imogene and love for his daughter were balancing each other out. Although it wouldn't take much for the burning ball of anger in his belly to explode. Layla gave a tiny wave, before yawning and snuggling down in his arms. If his brother had been shocked initially, he was even more shocked after seeing his daughter's face.

"Hi, Layla," Parker said and lightly brushed his hand over the top of her hair. "She's got your eyes and our dimple." He touched the indentation on his own chin. Yep, he and Parker were two peas in a pod, their facial features almost identical, even though Parker was two years older than him. The only difference was, Bird had inherited his mother's green eyes and Parker's were blue.

"I know she's mine." Most men would demand a paternity test, and he was surprised Parker wasn't suggesting he get one and not just take things on face value and Imogene's word. Maybe his brother would when they were alone and Imogene wasn't nearby. He'd cross that bridge when and if it happened, because right now he didn't want to go back to Parker's place. He wanted to see the house where his daughter and wife were living. Shock at how dramatically his world had changed in a matter of minutes was also settling over him. Maybe he was being naïve in accepting Imogene's declaration that Layla was his, but how else could he explain the instinctive feeling that she was a part of him. Just like he trusted his instincts when things were about to go FUBAR on a mission, he trusted what his instincts were yelling at him now with regard to his daughter.

Bird glanced over at Imogene. She'd remained quiet through the whole interaction. Her fingers were clenched together tightly and he could make out the slight movement of her cheek as she chewed on the inside of it, a sure sign the situation was causing her stress. Well, it wasn't easy for him either. He hadn't forgotten a thing about her over the last two years and now he'd missed out on so much. There was so many things they needed to talk about. The way she looked, petrified her world was crashing around her, also solidified his conviction that Layla was his.

Parker shoved his hands in his pockets and cleared his throat. Clearly he didn't want to hang around and Bird couldn't blame him. If the roles were reversed, he'd want to give Parker the space he needed to sort his life out. "I'm going to get back to the guys. If you need anything, bro, let me know.

"Thanks. Don't wait for me, okay?" He kept his gaze trained on Imogene as he spoke to his brother. The second the implication of what he said sank in, her eyes widened, a hint of fear making them darker as she wrapped her arms around her waist. He hated that he'd caused her pain, but fuck, she'd kept the knowledge of his daughter from him for two years. She deserved to be a little uncomfortable.

Parker nodded and walked off, back to where most of the firefighters from his station were congregated.

"Are you ready to go?" he asked Imogene as he checked on the baby in his arms. She'd fallen asleep and his heart somersaulted at the sight of her mouth pursed like she was about to blow kisses. Her fine, light-brown lashes rested against her cheeks. She was so innocent. He'd become a SEAL to protect the innocent and the baby in his arms reinforced his decision to do whatever was necessary to keep the world safe.

Love for her threatened to bring him to his knees. He

never wanted to let her go. He was due back on base in two days. How was he going to be able to catch a plane and leave his heart here in San Antonio?

He couldn't. There was no way he could walk away without his daughter. He had two days to convince Imogene to come home with him.

"Can I have my daughter, please?"

No.

The word was on the tip of his tongue. He'd only held her for a few minutes and Imogene wanted her back? He tightened his hold and Layla gave a little squeak in his arms. Fuck, the last thing he wanted to do as hurt her. Hadn't he just promised himself he'd do everything to protect her? That he wouldn't harm a hair on her head?

But he also wasn't going to keep mother and daughter apart. "How about I carry her to the car and then we can go back to your place and talk."

Like him a few seconds ago, he could practically see the word *no* on the tip of her tongue. Funny how a person's instinctive response was "no" in certain situations.

"Fine." Like she really had a choice, and he figured she'd come to that conclusion herself. "Let's go. I need to get my stuff." She headed in the same direction as Parker had only moments ago.

Giving her a minute to compose herself, he hung back, enjoying the heavy weight of his daughter in his arms. He didn't think he'd ever get tired of holding her. When Imogene stopped by a man, who then put his arm around her shoulders, a red haze clouded his vision and a growl erupted from his throat.

No one touched his wife.

Bird ate up the distance between where he'd been standing and where Imogene stood, in a few seconds. "Immy, Layla needs to get to bed." His nickname for her rolled off his tongue and he glared at the man next to her, his anger returning when the stranger didn't remove his arm from around her. If anything, he squeezed her shoulder in support. Or was it something else?

"Who are you?" the guy demanded as if he had every right to be touching his wife.

"Imogene's husband and Layla's father." He ground the words out and, if he hadn't been holding his precious child, he'd have had the guy in a chokehold before he could've blinked.

"Husband? Imogene doesn't have a husband. He left her."

Is that what she'd been telling people? That he had left her, when in fact it was the other way around? As hard as it had been, he'd told the guys on his team that his wife had left him. They were all single, and they'd sympathized, but didn't know the hurt that Bird kept buried deep within him. The knowledge that somehow he'd failed Imogene. He hadn't been enough to make her feel confident in their marriage.

Well, things had changed now, and he was going to do everything he could to keep his wife happy.

Now that she was only inches away from him, he wasn't going to let her go.

* * *

THE SHOCK that had held her in its thrall at seeing Leighton and sharing her secret was beginning to fade.

Now Imogene was aware that if she didn't diffuse the situation between Leighton and Brent, it could escalate pretty quickly. Although Leighton still held their daughter, no way would he put her life in danger to get in a fight. Then again, Leighton could probably have Brent on his knees with one hand, while still keeping Layla safe.

"Brent, it's fine. Yes, this is my husband. I didn't... umm...seeing him here is a surprise."

Brent cut a hard gaze at her and she gulped, taking a step back at the venom in her neighbor's eyes. She hoped to God the anger wasn't directed at her because she'd done nothing to give him the impression that there was a chance of anything growing between them.

"Really? So he just shows up and you're going to take him back like that?" He snapped his fingers and Leighton growled again. In the midst of all the chaos that was her life at the moment, she couldn't deny that the sound was sexy.

Yes, coming to this picnic had been a huge mistake all around. Although she wouldn't forget the look of complete adoration in Leighton's eyes as he gazed at their sleeping daughter. She remembered that look, only it had been so focused on her that he could practically strip her without lifting a finger.

Her heart fluttered and her body warmed in memory of just how intense Leighton's love for her had been. He'd put her on a pedestal, treated her like a queen, and it had been so hard for her to take sometimes. She was far from perfect, even though Leighton seemed to think she was. That pressure, along with his job, and the worry that every time he left, he wouldn't come back, had brought her to the point where she just...broke.

Imogene slammed the door shut on those thoughts. She needed to concentrate on the next couple of hours, although what she'd been thinking right now is what led up to the situation she now found herself in.

"Please, Brent, this isn't easy, and there are things you don't know."

He looked like he wanted to say more, but Leighton put himself between them. "Listen, I don't know what's going on here, but Imogene is my wife and I take care of my own."

"Haven't seen any evidence of that," Brent responded somewhat belligerently.

"Oh my God, stop it, the both of you. I've got one child, but right now it feels like I have three." She stepped around Leighton so she could look at Brent. "I appreciate what you're trying to do, but it's not necessary. I'm quite safe with Leighton. He won't hurt us."

Brent's eyes narrowed like he wanted to argue further, but she stopped him with her best "mom look". No doubt Leighton's expression wasn't friendly either. After a silent battle, he shrugged. "Fine." He pouted for a moment before pasting a smile on his face. "I'll pop over later to see if everything's okay."

Leighton laid a hand on her shoulder. "No need. As Immy said, I'll keep her and Layla safe."

Immy.

This wasn't the first time he'd called her that since Layla had literally run into him. It still had the power to turn her insides to jelly. Hell, everything about Leighton had her discombobulated at the moment. Seeing the way Layla had curled into his chest brought back memories of all the times she'd placed her own head over his heart.

The strong, steady rhythm had reassured her that he loved her.

"Leighton's right, there's no need, Brent. Thanks again. I'll see you later."

She grabbed Layla's stroller and, when she went to pick up the large diaper bag, a tanned arm beat her to it. With a quick flick, the bag was over Leighton's shoulder. "I can take it. It looked heavy."

Imogene rolled her eyes. "I've been carrying it all by myself for the last year and a half. I can assure you I would've been able to carry it."

His lips thinned at the reference to her doing everything by herself. "Well, now that I'm here, you don't have to do it all."

The safest thing would be not to argue with him, since they'd likely be doing that in about thirty minutes' time when they got to her house.

It didn't take her long to get to her car. It wasn't the prettiest car and had seen better days, but it got her and Layla from A to B. It was mechanically sound; she'd made sure of that before she'd purchased it.

A quick look at Leighton showed that, if possible, his lips thinned even more, revealing that he wasn't impressed with what she drove. Too bad. She'd done the best she could with what she'd had.

Yes, the reason she'd struggled was because she'd walked away from him. But that was beside the point, and he had no right to judge her. He waited silently while she folded the stroller and stowed in the trunk. When he handed her the diaper bag, she made sure her fingers didn't touch his. Touching him had gotten her into trouble from the second they'd both reached for the can of tomato soup in the store at the same time.

Leighton's touch was lethal, wonderful, and she'd missed it so much.

"Give her to me," she demanded when she had the back door open.

"Don't you think it would be better if I put her in her seat instead of jostling her unnecessarily by transferring her from me to you?"

"You don't know how the straps work on the car seat."

"No, I don't, but that's not my fault, is it?" The accusation was clear in his tone—he didn't know because she hadn't given him a chance to learn.

"I'm not going to do this with you where everyone can see." She clenched her fists to stop herself from slapping her palm on the top of the car in frustration. Leighton made a valid point that jostling Layla wouldn't be good. She let out a breath. "Place her in gently and I'll work the harnesses."

She stepped to the side to allow him access into the small space. He moved smoothly and deposited their daughter in her seat. Layla stirred and Imogene slapped her hand over her mouth to hold back a cry when Leighton gently brushed his lips over Layla's forehead. She thought she heard him whisper *Daddy's got you*, but she couldn't be sure.

He gave her room to deal with the safety harness and, a few seconds later, when she straightened, she found Leighton standing close. If she leaned forward she could lay her head on his shoulder like Layla had. But what would Leighton do? Would he reject her or hold her close?

Imogene didn't want to find out, so she sidestepped around him and went to open the driver's side door.

"I'll drive," he said quietly, right behind her.

God, save me from alpha men. "Uh, no, you won't. You don't know where I live. You don't know San Antonio. And it's my car, so I'll drive." She crossed her arms and lifted her chin.

For a few seconds, his lips lifted in a small smile and his green eyes sparkled. Then, as if he realized what he was doing and remembered everything she'd done to him, the smile disappeared and the sparkle dimmed like a fading shooting star. "Fine."

He strode around to the other side of the car and opened the passenger door. Imogene took a couple of deep breaths before she got in.

This drive wasn't going to be any fun at all.

CHAPTER 3

Bird paced the small living room while Imogene changed Layla. The soft sound of his wife talking with their daughter did nothing to cool the anger that had been simmering in him since he discovered he was a father.

All the drive back to the house, he'd been doing calculations in his mind. Working out that she must have been pregnant when she'd walked out on him. They'd been married for five years when she disappeared. They'd talked about kids early on in their marriage, but Imogene had wanted to wait. She'd only been twenty-two when they got married. And to be honest, he hadn't been ready either.

Bird let his mind drift back to their courtship. It had been fast but he'd known the second their hands touched in the grocery store that she was it for him. He'd thought Imogene had felt the same. They'd been married within six months of meeting.

The first few years had been wonderful; they'd been happy and, well, he was selfish enough to admit he hadn't wanted a child to spoil what he and Imogene had created. They'd been arguing one night, and he couldn't even remember now what it was about, because they didn't fight much. But he recalled saying he liked it just being the two of them. He hadn't liked to share her then. Such a dick move.

"Fuck, where did it all go wrong?" he muttered to himself. He hadn't been a SEAL when they'd gotten married, just an enlisted sailor. But then he'd decided he wanted to be a SEAL. He'd wanted to do more with his career. He'd given it everything he had and had survived BUD/S training. If he closed his eyes, he could still see the look of pride on Imogene's face when he'd received his trident pin. Their connection and marriage that night seemed stronger than ever.

"Dada," Layla's sweet voice dragged him from the trip down memory lane he was taking, and he was glad for the jolt.

Then the word she said registered. *Dada*. A wave of love and emotion swept over him again. He bent down so that he was on the same level as her. "Yeah, baby, I am your daddy." He pulled her in for a hug, but after a second, she squirmed, so he let her go. She patted his cheek, then toddled off to the corner where a dollhouse was set up. She plopped down on her diaper-clad bottom and proceeded to play with her dolls.

He could've stayed there for hours, just soaking up the fact that he had a daughter. That he was a dad. That he and Imogene had created a perfect little human being.

"I should've been there from the beginning," he muttered. The anger he thought he'd had under control flared to life again, and he clenched his fists to stop himself from punching a hole in the wall. But he wouldn't scare his daughter. He would do anything to protect her. "I should've been there to see your first smile. To hold you when you cried. To see your first step. Hear your first word."

"I'm sorry, Leighton. So sorry." Behind him he heard Imogene's whispered plea, but he couldn't turn around. His emotions were too raw. Too close to the surface.

He didn't know how long he stayed squatted on the ground, watching Layla play. Watching as she babbled to her dolls. Watching as the love for his daughter grew larger and larger with every passing second.

He was aware of Imogene behind him. He'd heard the soft fall of her footsteps as she crossed the room. The rustle of the fabric as she sat on the couch. The occasional sniff she tried to hide.

As much as he didn't want to address the issue, he couldn't put it off. He faced life-and-death situations on a regular basis. This wasn't that type of situation, but it was life changing. A line had been drawn in the sand.

He stood, walked over to his daughter and brushed a hand over her soft hair, the strands so fine and delicate. He then turned and faced Imogene. "Is there some place we can talk?"

Imogene twirled a lock of her hair, round and round, a nervous habit he'd found endearing in the past. He still did. And part of him hated the fact he was making her nervous. She was his wife, and surely she knew he'd never hurt her.

But circumstances were different now. They were both different people.

Eventually she released the lock of hair she'd been torturing and stood. "Yes, we can go to the kitchen."

"And we'll still be able to see Layla?" Bird didn't want his daughter out of his sight.

"Yes. It's why I chose this house."

He nodded and, for the first time since he'd walked in, looked around the space where his wife and daughter lived. There was the couch Imogene had been sitting on, and two armchairs angled toward the fireplace, where a television was mounted on the wall. A corner of the room was allocated to Layla's toys.

It wasn't display-home clean, but considering that a young child lived there, it was neat and tidy. Homey and comfortable, it reminded him of the house they'd lived in, in Riverton. Is that why she'd chosen this place, because it reminded her of their life together?

Now he really was reaching for scenarios that were a little farfetched, even for him. A lot of houses looked similar in their layout and design.

"Can I get you something to drink? I've got water or juice."

"No Coke?" he teased, surprised that the words popped out. Imogene's love of the caffeinated beverage was something he'd always joked with her about. Some people needed coffee to get through the day; Immy had needed a Coke at least twice a day.

"I gave it up when I was pregnant with Layla."

"Oh." Another thing he'd missed. Fuck, he could go on and on about all the things he'd missed over the last two years. "I'll just have a water then."

"Why don't you take a seat?" she pointed to the small

table with two chairs tucked up against the window. The view was of a neighbor's house. Did that house belong to Brent from the picnic? Best not to ask that right now, even if Bird wanted to know so he could make sure the other guy saw him in Imogene's house and knew she was off-limits.

"How long have you lived here?" he asked.

"Moved in about six months ago," she said as she sat and pushed the bottled water across the scratched tabletop.

"Where did you live before that?"

She sighed. "I'm sure you don't want the complete rundown of every place I've lived. So why don't you ask me what you really want to know?" Again she lifted her chin, as if daring him to challenge her.

Anger and desire for his wife vied for supremacy in him. Desire won out and ignited low in his belly, traveling down until his dick twitched against his zipper. Imogene looked even more beautiful than she had the last time he'd seen her. Motherhood had softened her facial features. She'd put on a little weight and she looked healthier.

The thought killed the kernel of desire. Was she better off without him? Was she happier not having him in her life?

No, he wouldn't let that thought take root.

"I guess the biggest question is why? Why did you walk out while I was away? Why didn't you get in touch with me when your note said you would?"

"I…" Imogene picked at the label on her water bottle. He knew the questions were uncomfortable, but she couldn't be surprised that he would ask them. "I'd planned to."

She'd planned to? That had to mean she'd decided not

24

to in the end and that she really wanted to disappear and not be found. How had she ended up in San Antonio, of all places? His Imogene loved the beach. There weren't any beaches in close proximity to the house they were sitting in.

But she wasn't his Imogene anymore. Had she ever been?

"What stopped you? Did you know you were pregnant when you left me?"

"Mama. Mama, dink." Layla scampered over and tried to climb up on Imogene's lap. His breath caught at the smile on his wife's face. The first genuine smile he'd seen on her since they ran into each other at the park.

He should feel annoyed that their conversation was being interrupted, but he couldn't. Not when seeing mother and child together smiling at each other warmed his soul.

"I can get the drink. What will she have?" He stood before Imogene could even lodge a protest. She had to understand that she wasn't alone anymore. That he was always going to be in her and Layla's lives now.

SEEING Leighton jump up to help shouldn't have surprised her. Hell, he hadn't even blinked when Layla interrupted their conversation. Unlike her parents, who'd always made her feel like a second-class citizen when she ever needed or wanted anything. She was always an inconvenience to them. They would've hated Leighton. Her parents had hated anything to do with authority or law enforcement and, while Leighton wasn't a police officer, he was military and a Navy SEAL, to boot. Of course, when they'd met, he hadn't been a SEAL, but still in the military. As ingrained as her parents dislike was in her, something about Leighton had pulled at her enough to forget about his career—until it became too much for her.

She closed the door on thoughts of her parents. Nothing ever good came from thinking about them. She should be thanking her daughter for the interruption—it had saved her from telling Leighton everything that had happened when she'd walked away. Oh, she knew she couldn't avoid the questions, but she would damn well try.

Imogene glanced up to find him studying her, and the desire to escape, to wish that the last few hours hadn't happened, almost consumed her. "Umm, in the fridge is a blue sippy cup full of juice."

"On it."

Quicker than she would've liked, Leighton was back and handing Layla her cup.

"Tank oo."

"You're welcome, sweetheart." He sat down and looked at her. "She can say *thank you*."

"Yes, she can." Pride swelled in Imogene at how she didn't even have to prompt her child to use her manners. She'd worked hard with getting Layla to try and say *thank you* instead of *ta* even though people thought her silly for doing it. But she and Layla had shown them what they could do as a partnership. Although she suspected, with Leighton looking larger than life in her kitchen, it wasn't going to be the two of them anymore.

They sat quietly together for a few moments, Layla slurping and Leighton unable to take his eyes off his daughter. The longer he looked at her, the less chance he'd bring up the thread of conversation they'd been working on when Layla interrupted them.

When Layla finished her drink, she squirmed and Imogene placed on the ground, her heart bursting with love as she toddled back to play with her toys. She'd have to think about dinner soon, and then there was bath time. Would Leighton want to stay and help?

Did bears shit in the woods?

Of course, he'd want to stay around. She suspected that if he'd been staying with his brother, he wasn't going to want to stay there now. But she couldn't let that happen. She couldn't let Leighton stay at her place, imprinting himself on her house.

"Talk to me, Immy. We have to sort this out before we can move forward."

She sighed and wished she had some wine but, like Coke, she'd given it up when she'd found out she was pregnant with Layla. "I know, but I don't know where to start. Or what to say."

"All I want is the truth, even if I'm not going to like it. I asked if you knew you were pregnant when you left me. That would be a good place to start."

"I didn't know that I was carrying our child when I made the decision to walk out." Imogene thought back to the night when it had all been too much and she'd left the house they were starting to make a home. Leighton had been gone so long and the Navy wasn't telling her anything. She'd known they couldn't because he was a SEAL and their missions were top secret. But the memories of the time when her parents told her they were going to the store, but they hadn't come back for three weeks, came crashing back on her.

They'd left her alone and, when the food ran out, she'd waited behind the only diner in town to try to get whatever scraps they threw out. How she'd never gotten attacked walking home in the dark astounded her. The town she'd grown up in hadn't been one of the safe, homey places in rural America portrayed on television.

She'd been too afraid to call the police. Her parents dislike for them was legendary around Roots Flat—even the cops knew it, so if she did call, they weren't likely to come to her rescue. Her parents had almost looked disappointed that she was still in the house when they'd returned from wherever they'd been. Over the years, they'd abandoned her on a few other occasions, but by then, she'd worked out how to cook and had made whatever food they'd left in the house last as long as possible.

"I'd never been so scared or as freaked out as I was while you were away on that particular mission. The previous times had been hard, but I'd coped. Or maybe I didn't and it just built up inside me. There was just something about this one that affected me more. Some instinct screaming in me that you were in constant danger and I'd never see you again. Every time the phone rang, I jumped. When a telemarketer knocked on the door, it sent me over the edge. I thought it was someone from the base coming to tell me you'd been killed. I didn't want to be left behind again, so I...ran."

She choked back a sob, but when Leighton made a move to comfort her, she held up her hand. She couldn't deal with him touching her. If he did, there was no way she'd be able to keep talking.

"Looking back, I can say it was probably my pregnancy hormones, along with past anxieties from my childhood, which caused me to freak out. I was all alone with my thoughts. I didn't have any friends to talk to about what I was going through. The people I worked with didn't understand and I didn't try to explain the rush of emotions enveloping me. None of the guys on your team had a wife or even a serious girlfriend I could hang out with. Someone who felt the same fear as me."

"Shit, Immy, why didn't you talk to me? Why didn't you wait?"

She sighed, hating having to relive the darkest period of her life. "I reverted back to the young girl who'd grown up in Roots Flat. You'd been gone six weeks and all I could think about was that you'd deserted me. That you'd come back and were living somewhere else. Irrational thoughts, but I couldn't stop them, so I ran, believing I was saving myself from heartache. I went to the bus station and got on the first bus that pulled in. I didn't even know where it was headed. For three days I went through the motions of living. Got off the bus when it stopped and got some food and drinks. Then got back on.

"I got sick when we were a couple hours out of San Antonio and, by the time we arrived at the bus station, I couldn't move. They had to call an ambulance. Turned out I had a bad case of the flu. While I was at the hospital, they ran a variety of tests, and one of them was a pregnancy test. As I had no idea I was carrying our child, they did a scan and it showed I was around eight weeks. I was numb and in shock. The last thing I expected was to find out that we were going to have a baby."

"Why didn't you come back then? Why stay away?"

One thing she loved about Leighton was his ability to listen without interrupting until the time was right.

"I'd planned to, as soon as I got out of hospital. But I was afraid, since we'd had that argument one night, and you said you liked that it was just us because after we argued, we could kiss and make-up without having to worry about being interrupted by kids. With my emotions running out of control, I was scared you'd tell me to get rid of the baby. Then I got the hospital bill and it needed to be paid. I decided I should get a job and pay some of it down before I headed back."

"What the fuck, Immy? I remember that fight but there's no way I'd ever tell you to get rid of the baby. You have to know that. Anyway, I was being selfish when I said that."

"If I'd been in my right frame of mind, I never would've had those thoughts. But I wasn't and so I did. I'm so sorry." It had taken a lot of therapy for her to come to terms with all this...only recently, even. Until now she hadn't been able to foot a therapist's bill on top of every-thing else. She'd lived with the dark cloud of postpartum depression lurking around her since Layla's birth.

Leighton blew out a breath and then she could see him taking a few more deep ones. She waited for him to say more.

"Why did you stay to pay the bills? We have insurance. Why didn't you put those details down?"

Yeah, it would've been so easy to skip this next part, but she couldn't. "While I'd been out of it on the bus, the person sitting next to me stole my wallet and phone. Until I regained consciousness, I was considered a Jane Doe."

Leighton's chair scraped across the floor and she

cringed at the sound. "Why didn't someone contact me then, as your next of kin? You did tell them you were married, didn't you?"

She'd made so many mistakes back then. So many *too stupid to live* moves that it was a surprise that she was still alive. "When I woke up, they asked me, and I told them I'd left you and didn't want to contact you. Then when I found out I was pregnant, they asked again, but I was in such a state of shock, I still said no."

Imogene watched him as he paced around the small kitchen, his gaze darting to the living room where Layla had curled up on her toy couch and fallen asleep.

I should put her to bed, forget about dinner.

She ignored the thought. Layla wasn't going to get into any harm where she was. Besides, when she finished her story, Leighton would no doubt walk out the door and leave them behind because of her stupidity.

"Anyway," she continued when the silence had stretched piano-wire tight. "I got a job, but then my blood pressure went through the roof and I ended up on bed rest for the duration of my pregnancy."

"Jesus Christ, Imogene, did you think to call me at any time during this period?" His anger pulsed out toward her, his fists clenched at his side. He looked formidable and if she didn't know that there was no way he'd harm a hair on her head, she'd be running for the door, scooping Layla up on the way out. The man standing in front of her was every inch a Navy SEAL.

"I did. I called the house phone, but found the number disconnected. I called your cell, but it went straight to voicemail, and I couldn't leave a message. I thought about calling the base, but I knew they wouldn't tell me if you were on a mission or not." She buried her face in her hands. Telling the story to Leighton was even harder than with the therapist. But Dr. Jordan would be proud that she was explaining everything to her husband. "Every move I made. Every step I took was the wrong one. But by the time I realized it, it was too late. After I was well enough and it was safe for Layla to travel, I caught a flight to California. Drove to our house but when I knocked on the door, a strange woman answered it. At first I thought you'd moved on, but then her husband came up behind her. I said I'd gotten the wrong house and walked away. To me, the message was clear—you'd sold our house, moved on without me, and that was it. I had to, as well. I returned here and made a life for me and Layla. There you have it," she said, needing to let him know that she'd finished.

He abruptly strode over to her. She leaned back in her chair when he stopped in front of her. "Pack your bags."

"What?"

"You heard me. We're leaving on the first flight to Riverton."

Leighton had lost his mind. That was the only explanation for his outlandish edict. She stood, pushing him away hard. He took a couple of steps back. "That's the most absurd thing you've ever said to me. I can't just pick up and leave. I have a job. A lease."

"I don't care." He ground the words out and his green eyes flared with a combination of anger and desire. "I'm not spending another minute apart from my daughter. Either you come with me or Layla and I go alone."

She staggered as if he'd stabbed her. Her worst nightmare was about to come true. Leighton was threatening to take her child away from her. No way was she going to let that happen. She'd worked hard to get on her feet after Layla's birth. Managed to get her mountain of debt from her hospital stay under control. Looked after her mental health. She wasn't going to lose her independence. And she wasn't going to run. "I know I was wrong, but from my perspective, you'd moved on. You can't expect me to uproot our lives because you demand it. I won't let you take my daughter from me. I think you need to leave."

"I don't think so."

She shook her head. Initially she was going to suggest he stay and help with Layla, but not now. He didn't have any right to come in and command that she return to California with him. She couldn't. "I don't care what you think. I'm not going to cave to your demands. As I said, I want you to leave."

They stood there staring at each other, both of them willing the other to back down, but no way would she. Not with her daughter's well-being at stake.

Just when she thought she might have to give in, Leighton looked away and blew out a breath, and it was as if all the fight in him evaporated with it. "Fine. I'll go, but this isn't over, Imogene. One way or the other, when I return to Riverton, I won't be going alone."

She gripped the back of the chair as he left the kitchen and went back into the living room. He squatted down and pressed a kiss against their daughter's cheek. Without looking at her, he strode out the front door. Imogene had no idea how he was getting home and she didn't care. But with the certainty of the sun rising in the morning, he would be back, and he wouldn't back down.

She had a lot of thinking to do.

CHAPTER 4

BIRD SUCKED DOWN HIS THIRD CUP OF COFFEE AND GAZED out the window, watching the sun break the horizon. A brand new day was beginning. Normally, he relished the sunrise. Loved running along the beach and watching the grains of sand turn from dark grey to a golden hue when the sun lit them up.

He and his team would be pounding those granules before storming into the cold surf and swimming two miles. He'd give anything to be back on the beaches in Riverton right now, but if he was, he might never have found out about his precious daughter.

Bird dragged a hand through his hair, knowing he'd fucked up. But he'd been so angry at Imogene. The world. But more importantly, with himself. He'd acted like a whiny kid who'd had his favorite toy taken away from him after Imogene left. The hurt and shock that she'd left him while he'd been away had taken a long while to clear. He'd been such an asshole most of the time, it was a surprise his team wanted anything to do with him. He hadn't been with them for long, but he was glad that they'd stuck with him and pulled him out of his funk. How many times had he'd been reckless on missions, not caring if he got wounded?

Now though, he was mostly angry that, instead of staying at their house, he'd moved out two weeks after he'd gotten back. It had been too hard to stay there where everything reminded him of Imogene, so he'd rented it out, fully furnished. Now he lived in a one-bedroom apartment that wasn't fit for his wife and child. He would have to give the current tenant notice. Fortunately, he was a single guy from the base, so he should be totally okay moving out on short notice. If it had been the couple that Imogene had seen, then things probably wouldn't have been so easy. But they'd moved out after only six months.

He made a mental note to call the guy. Maybe they could do a swap, and he could take over his apartment lease. Yes, that was a good idea.

"Did you get any sleep at all?"

Bird turned. Parker stood behind him, dressed in his work uniform. His brother was about to go into a two-day shift. The original plan had been for Bird to stay, but now he wanted to get back to Riverton as soon as he could.

"Nope." When he'd gotten home, the house had been quiet and he'd been relieved when he discovered that Parker wasn't home. Everything was still too raw and he couldn't even think about explaining what had happened since he'd left him at the picnic.

"Didn't turn out how you wanted it to, did it?"

Bird kept his facial features bland, using every trick he'd learned during torture training—never let the enemy see when they've scored a direct hit with their questioning. "Why do you say that?"

"Because you're here and not there, with your family."

Bird snorted. "Doesn't mean a thing. I could've come home to give her time and space."

Triumph lit up Parker's eyes and, in that instant, Bird knew he'd shown his hand. "I was right. What did you do? Or did she do something instead?"

As much as he didn't want to dissect what happened between him and Imogene, he needed some perspective and, dammit, advice. His brother could give him both.

"How long do you have before you have to be at the station?"

Parker peeled himself off the door frame and strolled into the room. "I have to leave in thirty."

Hell, he wished he had a little longer, but if he gave Parker the abbreviated version, it should be enough. "You're right. I blew it and I'm not sure how I can fix it."

"Tell me everything."

Bird spent the next ten minutes relaying what Imogene told him and how he'd demanded that she leave with him.

"That's some serious shit, bro. Do you believe her about her wallet being stolen and the sickness with the pregnancy?"

"Yeah. I do. You probably think I'm a fool to accept her word after she walked out and didn't contact me for two years. But I could've tried harder to find her. I know people who can trace phones in a blink of an eye."

"I don't think you're a fool, per se, but I think you need to be careful. Regardless of the overwhelming genetic similarities, you should at least do a DNA test to be one hundred percent sure. And as for knowing people who can do amazing things with computers..." He shrugged. "Sledge's wife is one of the best. She found Tory when she was kidnapped. But I have to ask, why didn't you want to find Imogene over the last two years?"

Bird turned away from his brother. In the past when Parker had asked him that, he'd always brushed it off and, thankfully, his brother hadn't pushed him. But now that Imogene was back, he couldn't ignore it. "Fear. Because I didn't want to accept that I'd failed as a husband. That I hadn't been enough to keep her happy. I loved her, and I didn't see that she was hurting. Fuck, I still love her, and isn't that stupid? After everything that's happened, I still want her and need her as much as I did when I first laid eyes on her." He reached up and fingered his chain, his thumb caressing the smooth surface of his wedding ring.

"Then fight for her. Do what you should've done when you got back from your mission and found her gone. You've got a daughter to fight for now too. You've never been one to give up, bro, so don't start now."

Parker had a point. Once Bird set his eyes on a goal, he did everything he could to achieve it. "But how can I do that when she all but kicked me out last night?"

"I hear groveling works well. And you were a bit of an asshole, demanding she get on the next flight with you. I know you have to be back on base soon, but do you think you can get some extra time? If you explain your situation, will they give it to you?"

"This is the Navy. I have no fucking idea what they'll do for me."

"Ask...what do you have to lose? If they say no, then you'll just be putting in a lot of air miles flying between

Riverton and San Antonio on weekends. I know you'll make it work, bro. I gotta run. Let me know what happens."

He came up to Leighton and they shared a back-slapping bro hug. "Thanks, Parker, I'll keep you in the loop with my movements."

"Later."

A deep shuddering sigh rippled through him. He had a shitload to think about but, before he could do anything, he needed to find out if he could get a few more days' leave. He didn't want to let his team down, but if he wanted to win Imogene back, that needed to be his focus. He just hoped they'd understand.

THE KNOCK WASN'T unexpected but, when it came, Imogene's heart triple-timed and her palms grew sweaty. She looked over to where Layla was sitting on her little couch, watching television. Sleep had been elusive last night, so she'd spent most of the night sitting in the rocking chair in her daughter's bedroom.

Thoughts about what Leighton would do raced over and over in her mind. Once her anger at his high-handedness had cooled, she understood where he was coming from, but she didn't like it.

Another knock sounded, only a little louder this time. Layla looked at her. "Door?"

"Yeah, baby, someone's at the door. Stay where you are, okay?"

"'Kay." She went back to watching her show and Imogene steeled herself to open the door to her husband.

Two years apart hadn't made him any less handsome to her than the day they'd met at the grocery store. If anything, his muscles seemed to have gotten bigger and there was a harder edge to him. All of that combined to make him even more attractive to her. She supposed he must have been on a lot of missions since she'd left. Had he been hurt on any? There hadn't been any visible scars on his arms, but that didn't mean he hadn't been hurt while saving innocents.

Imogene firmly pushed those thoughts away. She didn't want to think about Leighton's job at the moment, even though it had been a big reason for her running from him.

Smoothing a palm down the side of her jeans, she pulled opened the door. Damn...did the man ever look bad? His black hair glinted in the sunshine. His eyes were hidden behind dark sunglasses, but she imagined they were twinkling. In one of his hands was a gift bag, with a colorful teddy bear on the front. She didn't have to be a rocket scientist to know who that bag was for. In his other hand was a cardboard cupholder with two cups, and hooked over his arm was a plastic bag from her favorite donut shop.

Oh, he was going for the big guns. She hadn't had donuts from that shop for months, although he had no way of knowing that.

"I come bearing apology gifts," he said, an endearing smile on his face. Her stomach flip-flopped. She'd always been a sucker for that smile. But she had to remain strong. Make sure that if, and it was a big if, she went back to California with him, it was on her terms.

Oh, keep trying to tell yourself you haven't made a decision. You know you have.

She mentally shushed that scolding inner voice. "It's going to take more than coffee and donuts to apologize."

"I know." The smile wiped from his face and she felt a momentary pang of regret. He lifted his sunglasses, and she hated seeing the dull look in his eyes. "Can I come in, please?"

Stepping to the side, she waved him into the house. As he passed, she was assailed by the familiar musky scent from his favorite cologne. He hadn't changed his preference over the years and, as much as she hated to admit it, she still had a bottle of the cologne at the back of her bathroom cabinet. Last night was the first time she'd pulled it out to smell in months.

"Dada!" Layla squealed and ran up to him. Leighton held out the hot coffee and Imogene took it from him. A second later he had his daughter caught up in a hug.

"Hey, sweetheart, have you been a good girl for Mommy?"

She nodded and then squirmed to be let down. The second her feet hit the ground, she toddled back to her couch.

"How does she know me?" he asked. She was surprised he hadn't asked the question yesterday when Layla first called him *dada.* Of course he'd acknowledged it, but his mind had probably been in such a whirl with the news that he was a father, that what Layla had said hadn't fully sunk in.

What she was about to say was even harder than telling him what had happened after she'd walked out. "I wanted Layla to know you, even though we weren't together. I kept a picture of us in her room. When she was about twelve months old, I showed her the picture and told her that it was of us, her mommy and daddy. I did that a couple of times a week, until she could recognize you without me telling her who you were."

Imogene chanced a look at him, hoping that she wouldn't see anger and hatred in his eyes. To the outsider, it would be what she deserved. She'd known where he was, and if she'd tried hard enough, she could've found him. But she hadn't and, well, there was no point in continually going over what she should've done, but hadn't. He hadn't made an effort either. On that front they were equally guilty. Instead, Leighton was watching her, his face free of emotion; yet there was a fire in his eyes. Not anger, but a combination of desire and happiness.

A shaft of answering need flowed through her and she swiped her tongue out over suddenly dry lips. His nostrils flared and he went to take a step toward her, but hesitated, and remained where he was.

"Thank you. You didn't have to do that."

She sighed. He was being far too generous, as he'd been from the second he found them in the park. The only time he'd let his frustrations show was when he demanded she leave with him. "Yeah, I did. I ran out on you. Not the other way around. Layla needed to know her daddy is a good man. A man who risks his life time after time so that we can live freely. Her daddy is a hero."

"I'm far from a hero."

Giving into her baser yearnings, yearnings she'd been fighting since she'd looked up and found herself staring into his eyes again, she walked over to him and placed her hand on his arm. The muscles beneath her fingertips tensed before relaxing. "You are to me. And a girl's daddy should always be her hero."

He looked over to where Layla still sat. "I would gladly give my life to keep her safe."

"I know you would, but I hope you don't, because she needs you."

He reached out and brushed his fingers down her cheek, the touch unlocking so many memories she'd kept hidden away. "What about her mom? Does she need me?"

God, how easy would it be to place her hand on his chest, lay her head on his shoulder, and let him take all her troubles away. His lips were so close. All she would have to do was go up on tiptoe and they would be there, ready for her to take. Would he taste like he had all those years ago? Would her body still tingle in delight the way it had always done from the merest of touches? More importantly, did she want to find out?

Yes, she did, but she couldn't. It would complicate an already-complicated matter. She pulled away from him until there was at least five feet between them. "I do, but we can't. It's too soon, Leighton."

He straightened. His hand threaded through his hair before falling silently at his side. "You're right." He studied her for a few seconds more, testing her resolve, and it was so hard not to give in and tell him she'd changed her mind. "Our coffee's probably gone cold."

"Yeah, I'll warm it up in the microwave," she said, latching onto the safe, neutral topic. Picking up the tray from where he'd placed it, she went into the kitchen. Once the coffees were in the microwave, her head dropped and she concentrated on her breathing. The steady in-and-out rhythm calmed her blazing emotions.

Feeling more in control of herself, she straightened when the microwave beeped that it had finished. She looked over to the living room and her heart melted. Leighton had seated himself on the floor next to their daughter. From where she stood, it looked like Layla was telling her daddy all about the show she was watching. In return, Leighton was nodding and seemed to ask questions. When their daughter giggled and he leaned over and pressed his lips to the baby-soft skin of her cheek, Imogene imprinted the image into her mind, not wanting to ever forget it.

Last night she may have kicked him out and told him in no uncertain terms that he couldn't boss her around but, underneath it all, she'd known that going back with Leighton was the right thing to do. For the sake of their daughter, they had to work on their relationship. As much as it freaked her out and her heart constricted in pain at the thought that she might lose him anytime he went on a mission, she'd still rather they had a few months together than go back to the hollow life she'd been living before yesterday afternoon.

Forgetting the coffee, she marched into the living room. "We'll go back with you to California," she stated matter-of-factly, as if she were ordering a meal at a restaurant.

Leighton's head whipped up, quickly followed by his body, the movement so smooth, she had to wonder if it was one he'd practiced with his team. "What? Did you say you would come back to California with me?"

She nodded, too afraid that her voice would break if she vocalized her confirmation.

Once again he was at her side, this time his large,

warm hands framing her face. "You're going to come back with me? You and Layla?"

Him repeating the same thing should've been annoying, but if the shoe were on the other foot, she'd probably be doing the same. If she said it out loud, maybe it would convince him. Swallowing away the ball of fear and excitement lodged in her throat, she smiled up at him. "Yes, me and Layla. Your family."

He pulled her tightly into a hug and she automatically wrapped her arms around his waist. Contentment washed over her. The future wasn't set in stone. She might find that once they got back to California, nothing would work out, but at least they would have tried, and that's all that mattered.

"You won't regret giving us another chance, Immy. I promise."

And she silently promised that he wouldn't regret giving *her* another chance.

CHAPTER 5

AS THE PLANE CIRCLED TO PREPARE FOR LANDING, BIRD tightened his hold on the precious cargo in his arms—his daughter. She whimpered and pulled at her ears. He reached into his top pocket and pulled out a lollipop. While keeping his grip on Layla, he unwrapped the candy. "Here you go, princess, suck on that. It will help your ears."

The little girl grabbed it and stuck it in her mouth. Her whimpers settled down and he relaxed a moment before looking to his left at Imogene, who was gazing out the small window. Her fingers gripped the armrests so tightly, he could see the white of her knuckles. He'd booked the whole row because he didn't want to have to deal with a stranger in the row with him and his family. He normally sat on the aisle, so he could spread out. The center seat was always awkward. He also hadn't wanted a whole seat between him and his wife, so he'd sucked it up and sat next to her. Layla had spent the three-hour flight alternating between sitting on Imogene's lap or his. He couldn't believe the way she'd accepted him like she had, but he loved it, and he loved her.

With Layla a little calmer, he reached over and rested his hand over the top of Imogene's, squeezing it gently. "We'll be wheels down in about ten minutes; then, it will be all over."

She sent him a tight smile, but twisted her hand underneath his so that she could entwine their fingers. He'd been stunned by the changes over the last two weeks. It had been a whirlwind, but they'd sorted out her job and her rental house. The only hitch they'd hit closing off Imogene's life in San Antonio had been when Brent, her neighbor, had found out she was leaving. He'd tried to tell her she was making a big mistake, but Bird had shut that shit down fast by reiterating that they were married.

The other hard time had been when Imogene had said goodbye to her two friends she worked with. The three women had hugged for a good five minutes before Imogene had let go of them with promises of sending emails once she got settled.

He'd also contacted his tenant in Riverton and he'd been more than happy to do a housing swap. When Bird told the young sailor that the apartment wasn't as nice as the house, he'd reassured Bird that, so long as he could set up his gaming consoles, he didn't care. He'd already decided the house was too big for him, and had been thinking about moving somewhere smaller, so it worked out well for all. All of Imogene and Layla's belongings should arrive in a week or so. Once his tenant left, Bird had arranged for a service to come in and give the house a thorough cleaning. The house was going to be nice and fresh when they got there.

He couldn't wait to move back in. He'd hated living in the apartment, but the house without Imogene had been even harder to deal with. He'd also arranged a big surprise for Imogene and Layla—he hoped they'd like it.

Commander North had been accommodating when he'd contacted him about his situation. He said he would attempt to keep the team grounded, but he couldn't guarantee it as they were watching a couple of hot spots that could require immediate action.

Bird appreciated his commander's vow and, when he'd spoken to the team, they were happy with the possibility of staying stateside for a little while longer.

He imagined when he turned up for PT in a couple of days, they'd have a million questions for him. They'd stood by his side when he'd been dealing with Imogene leaving him, which he appreciated. He still considered himself the new guy on the team, having replaced Beck, who'd gotten injured while on a mission. The guy was now married to a Hollywood superstar. He worked on the base as a consultant, helping the new recruits, when he wasn't following his wife to various locations while she filmed.

The bump of the plane touching down had both his girls letting out little yelps of surprise. "See, I told you, wheels down safely."

Now that they were on the ground and taxing to the gate, the pinched look on Imogene's face relaxed and she exhaled. "Thank goodness."

He laughed. "I never knew you were a nervous flyer.

47

NICOLE FLOCKTON

You weren't that way when we went to Hawaii for our honeymoon. Well, not that I can recall."

A pretty blush bloomed across her cheeks. He hadn't seen her blush in years and he loved the sight of it. "Well, someone was keeping me occupied. I guess the fear of something bad happening to me, to us, got to me. I've got more to lose now."

Bird remembered their honeymoon flights and how they'd spent most of the time kissing and snuggling. He was pretty sure they would've been kicked off the plane if everyone hadn't appreciated that they were newlyweds. As for her other fear, he could understand that. He was relaxed because he flew a lot, but now he couldn't help wondering how he would be the first time he went on a mission, knowing that he had two people who needed him and counted on him waiting back home. He liked to think he'd be more careful, not take the risks he'd taken over the last couple of years.

"Ahh, yes, our flights to and from Hawaii were fun." He winked, then adjusted Layla, who was still happily sucking her lollipop. "As for the fear of flying, if anything happened, at least we would've all been together."

"Oh God, don't say that. From now on, I'm taking a train or bus if I have to travel anywhere." He opened his mouth to counter her argument but she held up her hand. "And don't spout facts about plane travel being safer than crossing the street."

He chuckled. "It's true, though."

Imogene dropped her head on his shoulder and he held his breath, waiting for the moment the penny dropped and she realized what she'd done and would move away. When she didn't, he exhaled and relished the close connection.

Right at this second everything in his life felt perfect. His daughter in his arms. His wife leaning against him. There was still so much they needed to sort out. So much to discuss, since they'd barely touched on what was going to happen. It had been easier not to discuss it while they were closing up her life in San Antonio.

The plane stopped its rolling—they'd reached the gate. With deft movements, he had his seatbelt undone and was standing, Layla secured to his hip, his backpack over his spare shoulder. Bird opened the overhead bin and pulled out the diaper bag.

"I can take that," Imogene said as she sidestepped toward him, her purse clutched in front of her.

"I've got it."

She huffed out, adjusted her bag, and clamped her hands on her hips. He bit back a smile, as he had a fair idea of what was coming next. "You don't have to handle everything. I've been doing this a lot longer than you have."

The last words were barbs to his chest, but he schooled his expression so she couldn't see that she'd made a direct hit. "I know, but I'm here now. You're not alone anymore."

Her gaze skittered away from him and, thankfully, the line of people began moving out of the plane.

"Come on, baby, let's get you home," he whispered to his daughter.

* * *

THE SCENERY WHIPPED BY, familiar yet strange. In the two years since she'd moved away, some of the shops she'd frequented were gone and different ones stood in their places. Restaurants had updated their awnings and signage.

The closer they got to the house she'd shared with Leighton, the tighter her nerves became. Layla had fallen asleep the second they'd pulled out of the airport. Somehow Leighton had arranged for his car to be left in one of those long-term parking facilities. Or maybe he already had it parked there when he came to see Parker. Even that didn't make sense though, because there was a brand new, top-of-the-line, in terms of safety, car seat in the back seat of his SUV. The one she'd brought with her from San Antonio now sat in the cargo area of the vehicle.

She closed her eyes and rubbed the bridge of her nose. There was so much that she wanted to ask him, but the words lodged in her throat, too afraid to erupt out of her. For a brief moment, after they'd landed, she thought they'd connected as a family. Then he had to go all alpha and remind her that he could not only carry his big backpack, but also their daughter and her diaper bag, all while not breaking a sweat. Imogene had seen the look of envy on the faces of some of the women on the plane at what Leighton had said and done.

A sigh rippled out of her and she shifted in the seat. This car was different from the one they'd had before she left. It was newer and roomier, as if he subconsciously knew he had a child. "When did you get this SUV?"

"About six months ago."

"What happened to our old car?"

He shrugged and checked the mirrors and over his shoulder before he changed lanes to exit the highway. "I was in an accident and the car got totaled."

"What? Were you hurt?" Her mind whirled and her stomach twisted at the thought of Leighton being seriously hurt or worse, being killed, and she wouldn't have known about it. Was it really any different to him being injured or dying on a mission? Was she still listed as his next of kin or had he removed her the second he'd worked out she wasn't coming back?

"I got a couple of broken ribs and a laceration on my arm. The car was old, so it was easier for the insurance company to write it off than to pay for repairs."

"How can you be so blasé about it all? You could've died!"

"The guy ran a red light. I saw him and swerved, but he still got me. It could've been worse if I hadn't taken evasive action."

"And that's supposed to make me feel better? Geez, Leighton, you had a serious accident. Don't brush it off as irrelevant."

"I'm sorry. I didn't mean to make light of it. It's just, you know, my job."

That was one thing she didn't need to be reminded of. There were too many nights she'd sat in her daughter's darkened room, watching her breathe, wondering if he was okay or if he'd died in some far-off country. In those dark hours, she always vowed the next day that she would call him, but when the day dawned bright, fear always held her back.

As if sensing the journey her thoughts were taking, he

reached across the console and placed a hand on her thigh, squeezing gently. Heat radiated through her blood from the simple touch, warming her and chasing away her ragged thoughts. A second later his hand was back on the steering wheel and she wanted to reach out, grab it and put it back. She curled her hands into fists to stop the urge.

The rest of the trip was made in silence, only broken up occasionally by a snore from Layla.

They pulled into the driveway and, when Leighton switched the engine off, her apprehension about getting out of the car went up a few notches.

The second she got out of the car, there would be no going back. Her life was going to be entwined with Leighton's again.

"We're here," he said quietly.

"Yeah, we are." Taking a deep breath, she opened the door and stepped out. The faint scent of the ocean drifted on the breeze and she closed her eyes, letting the familiar smell wash over her like a comforting blanket. She'd missed the ocean. Missed the ability to take a walk along the soft sand at the end of the day. How many times had she driven to the beach by the base to meet Leighton after work? They'd hold hands and talk about their day as the waves washed over their feet.

Would Layla like the beach? With two parents who did, she'd have to. At least, Imogene hoped she would.

A warm hand landed on her shoulder and her eyes flicked open. Glancing up, she saw Leighton standing beside her, Layla already secured in his arms. He'd taken to fatherhood as if he'd been born to it.

One of the fears that had held her back from

contacting him earlier was that he wouldn't want Layla. How wrong she'd been. Even Layla hadn't had an issue adjusting to the fact that her father was in her life. If anything, she looked more contented and relaxed than Imogene had ever seen her. Perhaps the little girl had known that a part of her was missing. That somehow the times she'd talked to her daughter about the man who was her father had taken root inside, lying dormant until the first time he held her and then it had bloomed to life, warming the places that Imogene hadn't realized were cold.

"Whatever you're thinking, Immy, stop. You and Layla are here now. We'll work it out." He pressed his lips against her cheek. This was the first time since he'd burst back into her life that he'd kissed her. A small kernel of need blossomed to life inside of her at the feel of his lips on her skin. What would he do if she turned toward him and grabbed his hand, making him stop? Then she'd reach up and brush her lips across his. Once, then twice. Would he recoil at her display of affection, or would he anchor her against his chest and kiss her as if he wouldn't be able to take his next breath if he couldn't have her?

Snapping herself out of her fantasy, and away from Leighton's touch, she turned toward the house, and the start of another chapter in her life. Whatever happened, she'd face it head on. The first time she'd lived in this house, she'd been a young wife. Now she was a mother and had faced hard times and hard decisions all by herself.

Following Leighton up the path, she noticed that the gardens were well-maintained, even though Leighton had been away from the house for a while. He probably had a service to look after the outside of the place so that, even while he was away, the house didn't get that look of *no one living there.*

He held the door open. She walked in and stopped as the lingering aroma of fresh paint wafted on the air. "You painted recently?"

He shrugged and placed Layla on the ground. "Welcome to your new home, princess."

Imogene watched as Layla looked around. She held out her hand toward her daughter and smiled when her little one slipped tiny fingers between hers. Together they wandered down the hallway, and Imogene embraced the sense of rightness about being back in the house that flowed through her.

This was home. And yet it wasn't.

Poking her head into the living room, she noted that the furniture they'd spent hours picking out was still there. Why was she surprised? Had she expected Leighton to dump everything they'd bought when she'd walked out?

Yes, that's exactly what she thought he'd do. She expected him to purge her from his life. After all, her parents hadn't bothered to stay in contact with her after she'd left home. They hadn't even bothered to come to her wedding.

She sensed Leighton walking up behind her. "Everything looks pristine and, like I said earlier, freshly painted."

"Well, I arranged for a service to come in and repaint, clean out the air conditioning ducts and steam clean the carpets and furniture."

"Why?" She was puzzled that he'd go to those lengths for her and Layla.

He sighed and rubbed a hand through his hair. It had grown in the last couple of weeks. She liked the longer length, but she doubted he'd keep it that way. "The place has been rented out for the last couple of years. I wanted to make sure everything was nice for you and Layla."

He'd gone to this much trouble for her? No, not for her, for their daughter. He may have included her in his explanation, but Layla would've been his priority.

Then his words sank in. He'd rented the house out for a couple of years? "Did you not live here at all after I left?" The words burst out of her. She hadn't meant to say them, but she was glad that she had.

Again, he shrugged, as if it wasn't a big deal, but it clearly was. "Let me show you the room I thought Layla could sleep in."

Imogene didn't have to guess which room Leighton was talking about. She would swear on her daughter's life that it would be the one they'd talked about being a nursery when they'd first looked at the house.

When he opened the door, her suspicions were confirmed. She crossed the threshold and her breath lodged in her throat when she saw what he'd created for their daughter. It was a room fit for a princess. The walls were a pale lavender and there were castle and princess motifs covering one wall. Resting against another was a white dresser, and the closet door had been repainted white, with a gold crown in the middle of it. The room wasn't huge, but somehow, whoever decorated it had been able to get a daybed, along with a crib, in the room. Both had matching lilac linens. She'd been thinking about transitioning Layla from her crib to a "big girl" bed, but thought she was still too young. Yet, somehow, Leighton had known what was needed for the future. That's exactly what this room looked like, a future where she and Layla stayed with him. A room she could grow into. The way Layla had plopped herself down in front of the dollhouse tucked into another corner and was already playing happily, it seemed her daughter loved it as well.

He'd told her he didn't want to pressure her, but what if things didn't work out? What if, like before, she couldn't cope and left? But it wasn't just herself she had to think about now. There was Layla and, already, father and daughter had created an unbreakable bond.

"What do you think?"

"It's beautiful. How did you get everything done so fast? This isn't something that can be done in a day."

"I called Ace, a fellow SEAL who's got three daughters and a son. He spoke to his wife, Piper. She got her girl-friends together and they went shopping. She hired a designer for me, who arranged for her team to work overtime to get the whole house done and ready for when we returned."

"That must have cost a fortune." Imogene walked over to the bed, reaching out to touch the comforter. The material was soft and good quality. Nothing looked like it was from one of those cheap stores that popped up, offering great-quality furniture for a fraction of a cost. Invariably, the furniture fell apart after a month. She had firsthand experience with those types of stores.

"You and Layla are worth it."

Was she though? She'd walked out like a coward. How could he possibly want to do this for her? Or create a room full of love for a daughter he'd known for less than a month? The answer was easy...he was Leighton Nelder, and he was a good man.

As much as she wanted to go over to him and hug him, she hung back. The future with him wasn't guaranteed and she had to make sure she protected herself and her daughter, in case everything collapsed and they were left alone again.

CHAPTER 6

BIRD STRETCHED HIS BACK IN PREPARATION FOR HIS FIRST PT in over three weeks. The guys on his team would punish him for sure, but he'd take it on the chin like the SEAL he was. The past two days had been chaotic. Imogene had settled herself into Layla's room. He slept alone in the master and wished he had the courage to go into the room where his wife slept, scoop her up, and carry her back to their bed. The main reason he'd rented out the house was because he hated sleeping by himself in the room that they'd created as their little piece of paradise away from the world. A place where they'd slept in each other's arms and told each other some of their fears and dreams.

Except those times hadn't been enough, since Imogene had obviously kept so many of her fears to herself. He'd been living in a fool's paradise, believing their communication was strong.

"Fuck," he muttered as he rolled his shoulders.

Going over and over where things had fallen apart

wasn't the way to fix them. Yes, they needed to be acknowledged, but dwelling on them could only create a greater divide between them than there already was.

Imogene walked around the house like the floor was made of eggshells, and nothing he said or did could make her relax enough to be herself. Fear lurked in her eyes on occasion and it killed him that he couldn't reassure her that he wasn't going to hurt her. That everything would be all right. How could he do those things when he didn't know them himself?

Layla, though, he smiled as he thought about his daughter. She was a whirlwind of energy. He loved to make her laugh and, when she curled up in his lap, the unabashed trust she exhibited toward him crushed his heart until he thought it was going to shatter into a million pieces. He would do anything to keep her and her mom safe.

"Bird, nice of you to finally join us."

Bird straightened and lifted his chin toward his team lead, Knox 'Fort' Porter. "Fort, good to be back."

"Everything all right?" Fort studied him and Bird willed himself not to fidget like a rookie on his first day of basic. He hadn't done anything wrong. After almost three years with the guys, and once he'd gotten his head out of ass after Imogene had left him, he'd proven himself to be a valuable team member. Yet, there were times he still felt like he wasn't good enough, and they wouldn't mind if he transferred out.

"Yeah, everything's fine. It's just been a crazy couple of weeks."

Fort nodded. "So I heard."

There wasn't much of a chance to talk after that as the

rest of his teammates arrived and they started their morning PT. His lack of continual activity showed a little on the run, but Bird pushed through. At the end of their session, he collapsed on the sand, his chest heaving.

"Feeling like a rookie again?" His teammate Silver plopped down on the sand next to him.

"Going for runs by myself isn't quite the same as the shit we do. I'll be fine tomorrow."

"So what's going on?" This came from Cricket and, when Bird looked up, he found that his teammates had formed a circle around him. A sign of unity and brotherhood.

He didn't know how much Commander North had told the others when he'd asked for extra time off. Their Commander was one of the good guys and Bird was pretty sure that all he would've said was that Bird wouldn't be returning as planned. Same with Ace...he wouldn't have told Bird's team the story. Before Bird had been assigned permanently, he'd filled in on occasion with Ace's team and a couple of others on base.

"I found Imogene while I was in San Antonio visiting Parker."

Hank whistled low. "Shit, that must have been a shock. Or did you know she was there?"

Bird snorted. "Seeing Imogene wasn't the biggest shock. And, no, I had no idea she was there."

"What aren't you telling us?" asked Fort.

"I have a daughter. Her name is Layla and she's the sweetest thing on this earth." He recalled what she'd looked like when he went in to see her and Imogene before he'd left that morning. Layla was spread out, one of the teddies he'd gotten for her tucked under her arm.

Imogene was curled up on her side, her hair covering her face. His fingers had itched to brush it aside and give her a goodbye kiss. But they weren't at that stage yet. In fact, they hadn't talked about their relationship since their return to Riverton, and it was something they really needed to discuss.

"How do you know she's yours?" Rocket asked, his voice hard. "You wouldn't be the first guy some woman tried to pass a kid off as yours, when it wasn't."

His hackles rose and Bird clenched his fists to stop from striking the man.

"Settle down, Rocket. I don't think Bird would be dumb enough to not get a DNA test or anything." Silver, the oldest guy on the team, said, diffusing the tension.

"I haven't gotten a test...yet." The guys groaned. "I said yet. I'm going to arrange one, but I don't need it. I knew the moment I looked into my little girl's eyes, that she was mine."

"I think I'd need more than just looking into her eyes to know," Rocket scoffed and kicked up some sand.

"I can show you her picture and once you see it, you'll see that a DNA test won't be necessary." Bird countered and stood. He could appreciate what his teammate was trying to say, but it was obvious to him that there was clearly something going on with Rocket. He'd been a bit short-tempered since his mother died a few months ago. He and the rest of the team had put it down to grief, but now Bird couldn't help wondering if it was something more. Something he hadn't told them.

"Wait here," he said as he gathered up the small bag which contained his microfiber towel and car keys. He moved toward the parking lot and his car, where he'd stowed his phone. Showing off his daughter wasn't a hardship and he was confident it would settle Rocket's doubts the second he looked at the photos.

Behind him he heard the soft footfall of the men as they followed him. He wasn't surprised that they hadn't stayed put. He reached his car and unlocked it. Once he got his phone, he opened up his picture app and flicked through.

Over the last two weeks, he'd taken multiple shots of his daughter as she played and watched television. He'd sat with Imogene as she read to Layla. The picture he wanted was the selfie he'd taken the other day. The resemblance between them was unmistakable. She was definitely his daughter.

Bird held out his phone to Rocket. "Meet Layla."

"Holy fuck," Rocket muttered and the rest of the guys peered over his shoulder. It was comical the way their eyes widened and flicked from the phone in Rocket's hand to Bird's face and back again.

"Well, I guess a DNA test isn't needed," Fort said after a while. "But I would still do one anyway."

Bird rolled his eyes. "I believe I said I was going to do that."

"So what's the story then? Are you and Imogene back together?" Silver handed back the phone to Bird.

"I wouldn't say we're back together exactly. We're working on things though." He quickly gave them the highlights of what had gone on over the last couple of weeks.

"Fuck, man, that's a lot to deal with," Cricket said.

"Yeah, it is. I'm giving Imogene space, because it's got

to be hard to be back in the house we shared before. Hell, even I'm having trouble sleeping there again."

"How did you arrange to be living back at your house?" Fort asked. "What about the guy who was living there? Where did he go?"

"We did a trade. He's living in my old apartment. When I phoned, he told me that he was thinking of downsizing, anyway, so he was more than happy to take over my lease. And we were on a month-by-month lease with my house, so as it was the middle of the month, I paid him back half his rent. The building manager at my complex was okay with taking my name off the lease and putting his on."

"That's some lucky shit right there," Rocket said. "Lucky shit indeed."

"Tell me about it."

They stood there for a minutes longer before Fort spoke again. "I'm guessing Commander North is aware of your change of circumstances?"

"Yeah, I phoned him the morning after I found out about Layla. Explained it and asked for the extra two weeks off. I've got to meet with him when I get on base to update him on the current situation."

"Right," Fort confirmed. "And speaking of base, time to get our asses home and then to work. Your daughter is beautiful, Bird. Don't fuck it up."

After a round of goodbyes, Bird climbed into his car, Fort's words echoing in his mind. The last thing he wanted to do was *fuck it up*, but until he and Imogene talked through things, it was entirely possible that was exactly what he'd do.

* * *

THE DOOR from the garage closed and Imogene knew that Leighton was back from his morning PT. She hadn't been asleep when he'd tiptoed into the room she was sharing with her daughter. The daybed was super-comfortable and Layla was going to love it when she moved from her crib.

She'd held herself still as Bird hovered by the bed. Her hair had been covering her face and she was grateful that he couldn't see how hard she was biting her inner cheek to stop herself from reaching out to him and asking for a hug. Part of her had hoped he would come into Layla's room during the night and take her back to the master bedroom and the bed they'd shared for so many years. But he hadn't and she hadn't asked if he even wanted her to share the room with him.

In the two days since they'd arrived in Riverton, Leighton had been nothing but a gentleman, giving her room to adjust to living in the house again. After they'd eaten dinner the first night they'd returned, and Layla was in bed, the memories of the despair and abandonment she'd experienced while he'd been away on that mission had crept in. She'd battled and pushed them away, determined that they weren't going to define her anymore.

Imogene was aware that they had to talk and that she should maybe make the first step, considering Leighton had been doing everything possible to make her and Layla feel welcome. Hell, he'd repainted the whole house and created a room fit for a princess.

Leighton walked into the kitchen and the piece of toast she'd been eating slipped from her fingers. His chest was bare and the shorts he wore for PT left little to the imagination. She'd been right when she'd seen him back in San Antonio. Over the past two years, he'd filled out even more. His six-pack was more pronounced and, while she'd known he was strong, seeing the evidence of his bulging biceps and wide shoulders made her mouth go dry. Her gaze skated over the puckered skin of several scars that hadn't been there two years ago.

"M-morning," she managed to squeak the word out. She pressed her thighs together in an attempt to stop the throbbing need coursing through her.

"Hey, you been up long?" He looked like he wanted to walk over to her and kiss her, like he'd done years before, but after one step, he stopped himself, like he remembered he didn't have that right anymore.

"No, not long." *Liar*, her inner voice yelled. She hadn't been able to go back to sleep after he walked out of Layla's room.

"Is Layla awake?"

Imogene looked at the oven clock. "Yeah, she probably is. You know how she likes to lay in her crib and chat to her toys before she calls out to me or you to come and get her."

His eyes softened and a sweet smile played across his lips. It was impossible not to see how much he enjoyed the role of being a father. "Yeah, she does. She's settled in well, hasn't she? I mean, this place is new to her, but she hasn't seemed frightened to be here."

Wiping her hands over her plate, she pushed back from the table. "She's woken a couple of times during the night, but I've gone over and patted her back for a few moments, and she's drifted back off to sleep."

Immediately, Leighton straightened and was by her side in a couple of strides. "She's woken up? Why didn't you come get me? You don't have to do this all by yourself now. I'm here to help you."

Without giving it too much thought, she placed her hand on his arm. "It wasn't a big deal. As I said, all she needed was to have back patted and she drifted off to sleep again."

She went to remove her hand from his arm, but Leighton's larger one covered hers. She looked up and swallowed hard. Shining in his green eyes was a combination of desire and possession. The same look that had been in them on their wedding day, seconds before they'd shared their first kiss as husband and wife. Her tongue darted out to moisten her lower lip and he groaned.

It had been so long since she'd felt the touch of his mouth against hers. During her time on bed rest while she was pregnant, she'd had many dreams of Leighton finding her and bringing her back to this house. He would kiss her, tell her he loved her and missed her. She'd always woken up longing for the dream to be reality. Now she could make it real.

"Kiss me, Leighton," she whispered, amazed at her brazenness.

He adjusted his stance and brushed away her hair with one hand while the other curved around her waist. "Are you sure?"

"I'm sure I'll hit you if you don't."

He smiled, the most open and free smile he'd given her since Layla had barreled into his legs at the picnic. If he hadn't been holding her rightt now, she would've fallen into a heap. "Far be it from me to deny your wishes."

His mouth closed over hers and she clutched at his shoulders. His skin burned beneath her fingertips. He was always warmer than her and she'd loved snuggling against him. The familiarity of his touch slammed into her. How was it possible that her body hadn't forgotten the way he kissed or the way he held her?

She angled her head, opening her mouth wider to deepen the kiss. Against her stomach, she could feel his erection. The shorts he wore didn't hide a thing, and she shivered. Liquid heat pooled between her thighs and she pressed herself closer to him.

His hand trailed over the thin T-shirt she'd worn to bed, his fingers bunching the fabric but not lifting it away like she ached for him to do. Her own hands trailed down his back, finding the elastic band of his shorts and slipping beneath. She squeezed his ass and his dick twitched against her belly. Her body was aflame with desire and she wanted to rip his shorts off and hold his hard length. Stroke him until he was pumping in her hand before he took over and drove into her, making her forget everything but just the two of them. She'd been so lonely the last two years without Leighton by her side. Being back in his arms reminded her of all that she'd deprived them both of.

She moaned when Leighton pulled his lips from hers. His fingers still gripped her T-shirt as though he didn't want to let her go.

"Immy, I've missed you so much." He pulled her tight against him and she relished being in his safe embrace.

"I missed you too."

He pressed another kiss to her forehead before stepping away. "I want nothing more than to take you to our bed and reacquaint myself with you, but I need to be sure it's what you want. There's still so much we have to work out."

His words cut into her, but he was right. "I know."

"Maybe tonight, when I get back from work, we can go out, the three of us. To the beach. Show Layla the ocean and get some take out and have a picnic."

"I'd like that."

"Good," he whispered before capturing her lips again in a soft kiss that was over much too soon. "I've got to get to the base. If you need anything at all, call me."

With one last hug, he disappeared out of the kitchen and down the hall. Imogene gripped the kitchen counter to stop herself from following him and joining him in the shower. What he said made sense. She'd walked out on him and their marriage. He may not have said it, but she needed to earn his trust again. And even though her body craved him, their relationship didn't need to be muddied by falling back into bed too soon.

CHAPTER 7

THE DAY WAS DRAGGING ASS AND FRUSTRATION FLARED through him every time Bird glanced at his watch, only to see that mere minutes had passed since the last time he'd looked. Watching the time had never been something he'd done, but today, his body and lips still burned from the kiss he'd shared with Imogene in the kitchen.

Her reaction to him had blown his mind and, while he was in the shower, he'd jacked off, wishing it was her hand stroking him to completion. The unspoken invitation to take her had been hard to reject, but he'd known that the timing wasn't right. Tonight he wasn't going to go to bed alone. Even though it would be hard, and he'd probably end up with a case of blue balls, Imogene was sleeping next to him from now on.

When he'd arrived on base, he'd gone straight to Commander North to speak to him about updating his personal details and adding Layla to his medical coverage. He'd never removed Imogene, even though he'd had no idea where she was. Once he completed that, it was a meeting with the guys about the most recent hotspot in a small African nation. Guerrillas were threatening the government and, as the U.S. currently had a Peace Corps group working over there, they were monitoring the situation.

The last thing Bird wanted to do was go on a mission when he'd just gotten Imogene back in his life, but if things didn't settle down, they were slated to be the team sent. Even though Commander North had said he'd try and keep them stateside for the next month. Sometimes that wasn't possible. The rest of his team had gone off base to get something to eat, but Bird had stayed and used the time to phone Imogene's favorite restaurant to organize the food for their picnic on the beach. Once he sorted that out, he headed for the commissary to grab a couple of items, as well as lunch for himself.

He was heading back when he spotted Ace, along with his teammates, Rocco and Rex.

"Ace," he called out and the other men stopped.

"Bird, good to see you. Everything work out okay?" Ace asked as they shook hands and slapped each other on the shoulder.

"Yeah, I can't thank Piper enough for everything she did in getting Layla's room furnished and working with the designer. It's perfect."

"Good news, man. When everything has settled down, come over and we'll grill on the deck while the kids play."

Bird was aware that Ace's girls were a lot older than Layla. They probably wouldn't want to play with someone so young. Although, there was John, their baby brother, but that was different. Babies were cute and everyone wanted to hold them. A stab of disappointment landed in his gut. He'd never seen Layla as a newborn. Held her. Burped her or held when she cried because her first tooth was coming through. And it crushed him that he hadn't been able to experience all those first-time-dad moments.

He pushed the thoughts away. He couldn't change the past, but he had a lot of other future milestones to share with his daughter. Aware that he hadn't answered Ace's questions, he nodded. "Yeah, that'd be great. Then I can thank Piper in person."

Ace laughed. "I'm sure she'd appreciate it but, honestly, she loved helping you out. I know Piper's keen to meet her, let her know that she's not alone."

"Thanks. I know Immy will value that."

They walked back to the building, chatting about inconsequential things. Once inside, they went their separate ways and, by the time Bird returned to the room where he and his teammates had been, they were back as well.

The second he walked in, they straightened, and he didn't like the look on their faces. "Fuck, don't tell me we're about to go wheels up?" He loved being a SEAL. Enjoyed the adrenaline rush of taking on the fucktards who thought they could lord over innocents. But right this second, he didn't love his job. Going away so soon after getting Imogene back was the last thing the two of them needed.

Fear gripped him that he'd return and find her gone again. But he squashed the thought like he'd squash a bug with his boot. No, she wouldn't leave. She couldn't.

"The situation we were monitoring has worsened. They've put us on alert for the next forty-eight hours."

Fort spoke decisively, as if he knew that was what Bird needed to hear.

"Right," Bird responded, not knowing what else he could say. He knew his job and what had to be done. People's lives were on the line. This wasn't the time to be selfish, no matter how much he wanted to be.

"Let's go over the location of the village and the latest intel. We'll talk about plans and work out the best location for drop in and extraction so we're prepared." Fort walked over to where he stood. "I know this isn't ideal for you, Bird, but it is what it is. We'd all like a little more time stateside."

"I understand. I know my job and all that it entails." And he did, but he just wished the timing wasn't so lousy. Hopefully, he'd still have tonight to spend with his girls. Explaining it to Imogene wasn't going to be easy, but she had to have known that this was a possibility when she returned with him. He just hoped that she wasn't going to regret her decision to give them another chance.

* * *

IMOGENE STEPPED out of the car and inhaled deeply. The scent of ocean and sand was stronger here than at the house. Such a nicer thing to smell than the fumes from the cars that constantly passed her house in San Antonio.

She turned to help Leighton get Layla out of the car, but she found that her über-efficient husband already had their daughter out of her car seat and was in the process of collecting a basket and Layla's diaper bag from the trunk. Her instinct was to say she could help but she swallowed it down. Instead, she took hold of Layla's hand, as she jumped up and down in excitement at being at the beach. She could at least do this, so Leighton didn't have to worry about doing everything.

For some reason only known to him, Leighton was determined to prove to her that he not only could step up and be a father to their child, but that he loved it as well. Most women would be happy but, for some stupid reason, she wanted to see something other than compliance in his emotions. He had every right to be angry with her for what she'd done. He'd shown her a glimpse of it that first night, but since then, he'd kept it buttoned down. She worried that it would all get to be too much and he'd explode.

Or maybe he's accepted everything and wants to move on. Can't fix the past but can make the future everything the past wasn't.

Her inner voice occasionally came up with words of wisdom and she should pay attention to it. Why cause trouble when there was no reason to?

"You ready, Immy?" He asked as he came up and slung his free arm around her shoulders. "How about you, princess? Ready to see the ocean."

"Yes. Yes. Bird. Bird." Imogene looked down at her daughter in surprise. How had she known *Bird* was her daddy's nickname? Beside her, the man in question chuckled.

"I think she's referring to the seagulls and not me."

Imogene looked up and saw them circling the blue sky. "Oh, of course."

His lips brushed the sensitive patch of skin at the base of her neck, and a shiver spiraled down her spine, like a slinky going down some stairs. "But it's sweet that you thought she was talking about me."

She rolled her eyes, hoping he hadn't noticed the way her body reacted to his proximity. "Come on, let's get to the water before the sun sets."

The reality of the picture they made was cemented in her when she spied their three shadows as they made their way toward the soft, white sand. Anyone looking at them would immediately think they were a family. Technically, they were, but they weren't a solid family unit. She worried that a strong breeze would rip them apart. That was the last thing she wanted. Now that they were together, she wanted them to stay that way. But for that to happen, she needed to work on herself. Work on her worries when Leighton went away.

Even when they were apart, fear threatened to engulf her, fear that something would happen to him and she wouldn't know. All she hoped was that it would be a while before he would have to go on a mission.

They found a nice patch of sand, not too close to any other family. It was summer, but this late in the day, most people had headed off home, and only a few groups remained.

"I think we should be good here, don't you, Layla?" Leighton plopped down on the blanket he'd just spread out.

"Leighton, you're getting sand on the blanket," she complained and reached down to give it a little shake.

"Immy, we're at the beach. Walking away not covered in sand would be a miracle."

She sighed and sat down on the blanket too. "I suppose."

He laughed and then surprised her by dropping a kiss on her lips. "I'd forgotten your love/hate relationship with the beach. You love to swim and soak up the sun, but you hate the sand."

"It gets in places it shouldn't," she grumbled, but was secretly thrilled that he hadn't forgotten everything about her.

"I'll help you wash it all away," he winked, but then stood. "Come on princess, let's put our feet in the water."

Layla squealed in excitement as Leighton effortlessly lifted her onto his shoulders. Not wanting to miss out on the fun, Imogene scrambled to her feet and followed them down to the water.

Layla was giggling and squirming from the cold water rushing over her feet by the time she reached them. She stood back a little, letting father and daughter have this special time together. Her heart burst with love and joy watching the two of them. She bit her lip and willed the tears building in her eyes not to flow down her cheeks. Her daughter was a combination of the best things from her and Leighton.

She shivered when a cloud suddenly covered the sun and she hoped it wasn't a sign that something was going to upset her little family.

Two hours later, after they'd had their fill of fried chicken and salads, she rested her head on Leighton's shoulder while Layla lay curled up in his arms. She'd fallen asleep on his lap and neither one of them had had the inclination to return to the car and drive home.

It was as if they both knew that this was a moment out of time, where the past hadn't happened and they'd always been this family.

"I suppose we should head home," she murmured after another few minutes had passed. Beside her, Leighton tensed. Every now and then, when she'd glanced over to him, his mouth was drawn into a thin line and his normally bright-green eyes were darker, as if he had a million worries weighing him down. "What's wrong?" she asked and pulled away from his side.

"I need to tell you something."

The food she'd eaten balled in her stomach like a dead weight. He was about to tell her that he'd changed his mind. That he didn't want to be with them. As much as her mind tried to reassure her that those thoughts were irrational, she couldn't shake them off. Why would he say he didn't want them when he'd spent a bucketload of money on fixing up the house? "What?"

"There's every chance that I might have to leave on a mission in the next forty-eight hours. We got put on alert today."

Her heart plummeted to her feet and she swallowed hard as bile burned the back of her throat. "Oh."

It's too soon. Way too soon for him to go away. She wasn't remotely ready to be alone in that house without him there. He may have painted, but that hadn't covered up her memories of those last few weeks she'd been there when she hadn't been able to contact him, and her thoughts had her imagining all sorts of horrid scenarios. Her fear of abandonment reared its ugly head, threatening to pull her under, drag her away from her second chance at happiness.

Leighton's hand rested over her clenched fists, his heat seeping through her flesh, warming her. "I know it's too soon, Immy. I wish I could ask that another team be considered for this mission, but I can't. I've just come back from three weeks' leave. I don't have that authority. I don't want to leave you and Layla, not now that you're both back in my life."

The pain at the situation was evident in his voice. "I don't want to lose you again," she whispered her biggest fear.

"You won't. I will do everything I can to make sure I always come home to you and Layla."

He never said the word *promise* and she couldn't blame him. She wouldn't ask him to either. But she could make sure that his mind wasn't back here in Riverton when it should be on the job. She had to remember she wasn't the same girl who'd walked out two years ago. Then she'd been a mass of emotions she hadn't been able to understand. Her black thoughts then weren't who she was now. Hours of therapy had helped her understand what had driven her actions. If Leighton was called away, she would get in touch with her therapist, see if they could do a virtual session, or she'd ask for a referral to see someone in Riverton. She wasn't going to go back, not after all the progress she'd made.

Reaching out, she touched his cheek, the bristles from his light scruff caressing her palm. "I know you will and you have to go. We'll be fine. I will be fine."

He studied her for a few minutes, as though trying to see if she was telling the truth or not. "Okay," he said, but part of her was worried that he didn't believe her, and that hurt. She supposed she deserved his wariness. After all, he hadn't known the way her thoughts had been all over the place back then. She'd never told him. Secretly, she'd always hoped he would notice and, when he hadn't, some of that resentment had been another factor in her running away.

The beauty of the evening and the closeness they'd shared over the last couple of hours had disappeared like the foam from an incoming wave. "I think it's time we got Layla to bed. We should bathe her, get the salt water off her, but that will probably wake her. Then again, if we don't, she's going to wake up gritty a—" Her words were cut off when Leighton's lips crashed down on hers.

Like it had always had the power to do, his kiss melted her on the spot. She softened and leaned farther into the embrace. Their tongues danced together before retreating, then coming back again. She wanted to climb into his lap, push him back so that he fell on the sand, and show him that she still loved him.

Saying the words out loud scared her. Too much time had passed since the last time she'd said them to him. Would he even believe her? Did he even still love her? Oh, he desired her…his moans and the way he clutched her head close to his showed her that. And she had no doubt that if she reached down in between his legs, the evidence would be hard against her palm.

He broke the kiss, both of them panting to fill their lungs with oxygen. "I agree it's time to go."

Not needing to be told twice, she scrambled to her feet. "You've got Layla, I'll clean up." When it looked like he was going to protest, she held up her hand. "You don't need to be superman and do everything, okay? I've got this."

He nodded.

Finally, a victory. A small one, but she'd take it anyway she could get it.

CHAPTER 8

LEIGHTON BOLTED UPRIGHT IN BED, THE KA-BAR HE KEPT in between the mattress and base in his hand, ready to strike out at whoever had walked into his room.

A squeal of fright cleared the battle haze that had enveloped him. "Immy?" He reached out and flicked on the lamp on the bedside table, blinking rapidly at the sudden brightness. "What are you doing here?"

"Trying not to be sliced."

"Fuck." He reached down, grabbed the sheath, and popped his knife back in it, before returning it to his hiding spot. "Sorry, I heard a sound and just went into fighting mode." He rubbed a hand down his face. "Is everything all right? Is Layla okay?"

After returning from the beach, he'd received his first lesson in parenting a grumpy toddler. Layla had protested from the second they'd gotten into the car. She'd woken up when they were heading back to the car and had wailed about leaving the beach. Even assurances from the both of them that they'd return hadn't been enough to stop Layla from sobbing. By the time they got her bathed and settled in bed, both of them were exhausted. Any plans Bird had to seduce his wife took a backseat to making sure their daughter was put first and her needs were met.

As much as he'd wanted to haul Imogene to their room, just to hold her, he could see that she was determined to stay with Layla. Even after their daughter had settled down to sleep. So, he'd retreated to his room, where he'd showered and fallen asleep.

All of that didn't explain why she was standing just inside his room, wearing a T-shirt that barely covered her ass. His dick hardened. Clearly, that part of his anatomy was wide awake and ready for some action.

"Layla's fine, but..." Her fingers fiddled with the hem of her shirt.

"But?" He tried to keep his mind off the hope that perhaps she'd come in to seduce him, after all. He kept his face impassive as she slow-walked toward him.

She placed her knee on the bed, leaning forward. His hand went to her waist, steadying her. "I'm not fine."

Her lips landed on his, the momentum forcing him back onto the mattress. His fingers threaded through her hair, holding her in place. God, he'd missed having her in his arms. Missed her welcoming smile and hug when he walked in after work. Missed her steady presence in his life. She had no idea how much having her by his side kept him focused and grounded.

He needed her like he needed his next breath.

As much as he didn't want to, he pulled his lips away from hers. "We need to talk, Immy."

She shook her head. Wisps of her hair brushed his

cheek and he pushed it away so he could see her. "I don't want to talk. I just want to feel, babe. I've missed this. I've missed you."

Everything in his brain was telling him to push the point that they should have a conversation before getting intimate. Sex always muddied stressful situations. But he'd fucking missed her so much and his hand had been a poor substitute over the last two years.

"I've missed you too," he said while he reached down and grabbed the hem of her T-shirt. She lifted herself away from him and pulled the shirt over her head. He drank in the sight of her naked body. He had wondered if she'd been wearing panties, and now he knew for sure that she wasn't. Her breasts looked fuller than he remembered and her stomach was slightly rounded. He placed his hands over her belly, reverently. She'd carried their child. Had nurtured her and brought her safely into the world.

Leighton leaned forward and pressed a soft kiss on her flesh before reaching up and bringing her toward him. "Thank you," he whispered against her lips.

"For what?"

"For Layla. For ensuring she was born healthy and continuing to cherish her into the beautiful girl she is." He closed the minuscule gap and poured all his gratitude and pride into the kiss.

Her flesh was warm beneath his fingers and her breasts were crushed against his chest. Beneath the sheets, his cock hardened even further. He wanted to forego all the foreplay and just sink into her. But that would be selfish and not how his wife should be treated after their time apart.

He shifted their positions so that they were lying side by side. Leighton pulled away and placed his hand on her cheek. "Are you sure this is what you want, Immy? Even with so much still unsaid between us."

Her hand covered his and pulled it away from her cheek. Disappointment lanced him like a dagger but, if she'd changed her mind, he would respect it.

"I know we should talk before we do this, but I need you tonight." She placed his hand over her breast and he sighed in relief—she hadn't changed her mind.

"You have me." He massaged the soft flesh while he found her lips again. Her moan as he pinched her nipple went straight to his groin and the need to possess her was almost too much to control. His cock was practically begging him to forget everything except thrusting into her and owning her again.

"I don't know how long I'm going to last, Immy. It's been so long."

"Me too. I don't care, babe. Just take me."

It was all the encouragement he needed. He pushed her back on the bed and covered her body with his. His mouth found hers again and they ravaged each other as if they were both afraid that they'd never get the chance to do it again. His hand trailed down the side of her body, moving across her belly until he found what he was looking for. Slipping his fingers between her legs, he tickled her pussy and she moaned, arching her hips.

He needed to taste her. Needed to imprint her back into his soul. The past two years, he'd lain in bed, wishing for this moment. In the darkest hours, he always vowed when he woke up, he'd search for her. Then daylight came and he didn't. Now, he never wanted to let her or Layla go.

He brushed his fingers across her belly as his mouth zeroed in on her pussy. He flattened his tongue and swiped her folds. Imogene's body arched off the bed and he clamped an arm over her to keep her still. He sucked, licked and nipped her clit and her moans grew louder and louder. Her thighs shook against his head, a sure sign she was close to her climax. He inserted two fingers and pumped while he bit down gently on her clit again. It was enough to send her over the edge and she shattered beneath him, her release coating his tongue. Bird closed his eyes and savored the moment. For a while he'd imagined he'd never get to experience this intimacy with her again. Bird had no idea how she'd feel in the morning, but he wasn't going to think about that. He was going to concentrate on the here and now.

As Imogene's body settled down after her orgasm, he kissed his way up her belly. Kissing the faint silver scars she'd gotten from carrying their daughter.

"Are you kissing my stretch marks?"

"Yes. They're your badge of honor and I love them."

"You're weird," she huffed.

He lifted his head to look at her. "Like my scars, they show what we've been through. I just wish…" He didn't say more as he didn't want to spoil the mood between them.

"Me too." Imogene cupped his chin and pulled him toward her.

He scooped her close and then rolled so that she was on top of him. Her hair fell around them like a curtain. They stayed like that for moments, their kisses saying all the things that needed to be said but both were too afraid to say out loud.

He found her breasts and massaged them. This was the best thing about the position they were in. He could play with her tits. God, how she loved it when he did. A low moan echoed around the room and she ground her hips against him, causing his cock to twitch with the need to be inside her.

Reaching out, he fumbled to open the top drawer of his bedside table.

"I've got it," whispered Imogene. A moment later her fingers closed around his cock. His breath hissed out as she started to stroke him.

"Fuck, I've missed you touching me." He closed his eyes and blew out a breath. If he wasn't careful, he'd come all over her hand, and that was the last thing he wanted to do. "Put the condom on, Immy."

"I've missed being able to touch you too. So many lonely nights."

His hips lifted when she slowly rolled the latex down. She was torturing him and enjoying it. He wanted to grab her hips and slam her down on his cock. But he also wanted Imogene to feel in control, do as much as she wanted, so he gritted his teeth and gave himself over to her and her ministrations.

"Are you ready, babe?" She asked, her slick center resting on the tip of his cock, her fingers tracing over a scar that he'd gotten while he'd been on the mission that changed their lives.

"I'm always ready for you." He groaned as she slid down on him. When she was fully seated, he made a conscious effort to relax his body.

Imogene rolled her hips against him and then began to move. His hands went to her waist, resting lightly, not taking over but letting her know he was there. She continued to slow-ride him and he loved every second of it. He reached up and plucked at her nipples, her rhythm faltering for a moment before getting back on track.

Her moans grew louder the faster she moved, her eyes never leaving his. The connection that had always been between them seemed to grow thicker, stronger, entwining around them in a shroud of desire and longing.

He reached behind her and planted a hand in the middle of her back, pushing her forward. Her breasts swayed in front of his mouth and he latched onto a nipple, sucking deeply. Her inner muscles clenched around him and he could tell she was about to explode soon. Her motions became more erratic, the closer she got to her release. Imogene slammed down on him one last time, her back arching as she moaned low and long and orgasmed around his cock. With her head thrown back, eyes closed, she'd never looked more beautiful to him.

His body ached for its climax. He hooked an arm around her, turned them so that he was on top, and began to pound into her, prolonging her orgasm. It wasn't long before he was shouting out her name as he came hard into the condom.

Bird collapsed on top of her, breathing erratically, but he'd never felt more alive than he did right this second. Leaning down, he kissed Imogene, pouring all his feelings into it, hoping she understood just how much having her back in his arms meant to him. He had to swallow down his words of love for her. That was the last thing she needed to hear right now. Not when there was still so much they needed to work out.

No other woman had ever tied him up in knots like she had. From the first moment he touched her, he'd been lost. Looking back, he could see that he'd rushed her into marrying him, but she hadn't seemed to mind. Their wedding in Vegas had been fun and, afterward, the rest of the weekend had been amazing. Now he couldn't help but think that if he hadn't rushed her, if he'd taken the time to build up their trust and communication, that things would've turned out differently. That she would've been more prepared for the uncertainty with his missions. Not only had they had to deal with being newlyweds, but he'd also gone into his vigorous BUD/S training, which was stressful and tiring.

Regardless of all that, and there really wasn't any point in playing "what if," he had her back in his arms and he wasn't going to let her go. Not this time.

CHAPTER 9

IMOGENE WILLED HERSELF NOT TO MOVE A MUSCLE WHEN Leighton's lips brushed across her cheek. The shift of the mattress, the loss of his warm embrace had woken her but she'd kept her eyes firmly shut. She didn't regret what they'd shared together last night. How could she when she was the one who'd instigated it all? When she'd been the one to walk into his room and throw herself at him.

If Layla hadn't been grumpy when they'd gotten home from the beach, the bedroom was where they would've ended up anyway. Sex and attraction was something that was never a problem between them. They'd had that from the beginning. Talking was where they'd fallen down.

Once the whir of the garage door closing echoed through the house, Imogene breathed out and threw off the covers. She remembered that Leighton would come home from PT starving and liked a full breakfast of eggs, bacon and sausage. The least she could do was cook it for him. She hadn't felt confident enough to do it the previous morning when he'd returned from his session, today she did. Unless his habits had changed over the last couple of years and he stopped somewhere else to eat.

Or maybe he stayed with his team now and they all went out to eat. He hadn't been with them long when she'd left. Had any of them gotten married or had a steady girlfriend in the time they'd been apart? It would be nice to have another woman or women to talk to when the guys went on missions. Maybe they could all hang out together.

Here she was thinking about a future when nothing had been sorted out between her and Leighton. There was still so much up in the air. He hadn't asked for a DNA test. He'd taken her word on face value and, well, there was no doubting Layla was his daughter, not with her dimple and green eyes that were the same as his. There wasn't much of herself in her little girl. While that had hurt her initially, the more Layla's features became like her father's, the happier Imogene had become, because she had her own little piece of Leighton that she could keep close to her.

A distance ringing jolted her from her thoughts and she sprinted into Layla's room, where she'd dumped her purse and her cell phone.

She grabbed the phone but just missed the call. Who would be calling at the crack of dawn anyway? It was probably some telemarketer from the other side of the world. No sooner had she finished the thought when her phone shrilled to life again.

Quickly she swiped it, not wanting the sound to wake Layla, although even with the time difference, it was still early for one of her friends to be calling her. Not that she had a huge number of friends, but there were a couple of moms she'd got friendly with when she'd taken Layla to the park. Not to mention Carol and Trixie from her old job, although she had those women in her contacts so if they called, their names would show up on her screen.

"Hello." Silence greeted her. Damn, it was a telemarketer. There was always a lag after she answered before the recorded message started. But she thought she could hear someone breathing down the line.

"Hello," she said again, a shiver of apprehension tiptoeing down her spine.

"Why?" The voice sounded a little distorted and she couldn't make out if the caller was male or female. Asking her *why* was definitely weird and confusing. Why what?

"Pardon?" Imogene rolled her eyes at what she'd done. Why the hell was she engaging with this person?

"Why?" They asked again.

Imogene disconnected the call, her heart racing as if she'd run a marathon. The call had to be a wrong number. She didn't know anyone who would ask her *why*. Pulling up her call log, she hoped that she could see the number the person called from and, if she recognized it, she'd call them back and give them a piece of her mind for trying to scare her. Unfortunately, her log showed the number as being blocked.

Could a blocked number be a wrong number or could it be something more sinister? And if it was the latter, who would be after her and why?

Okay, now she was beginning to get ahead of herself. Thinking terrible scenarios when she had no reason to. As far as she could recall, she didn't have any enemies. Yet she should probably tell Leighton about it when he got home. Of course, if she did that, he might go off the deep end and tell her to change her number. Or insist that she couldn't leave the house without him. No way would she be happy with either of those things. She'd survived by herself for the last two years and, just because she was back living with him now, didn't mean he had the right to dictate her every move. He would tell her he only wanted to keep them safe, but she was sure that it was simply a wrong number and would tell him so.

She glanced over at Layla's bed. Her eyes were still shut tightly and her diaper-clad bottom stuck up in the air. Her favorite teddy was tucked under her arm. She was the most precious thing in Imogene's world, and she would do anything to keep her safe.

So would Leighton, now that he knows he's a father.

She couldn't deny the truth of her inner voice. The last thing she wanted to do was hurt her daughter, but what she could do for Leighton was confirm that she hadn't lied to him about the paternity of their daughter.

A little snore emitted from Layla and she smiled at the sound. After covering her with a light blanket, she crept out of the room and to the bathroom. Once she had a quick shower, she'd get dressed and then start on breakfast. Even if Leighton decided to eat with this teammates, she and Layla needed to eat. The food wouldn't go to waste.

* * *

BIRD'S MUSCLES ached and he'd have loved nothing better than to stay in bed with Imogene curled up beside him. But, as a SEAL, his job required him to be in top physical condition and a day off could make a huge difference. Not to mention, he'd missed a couple of weeks while he'd been in San Antonio.

"Come on, Bird, you're dragging ass again," Fort barked at him as they ran along the beach.

Bird picked up his pace and ignored the soreness. A little pain was necessary when it came to saving people's lives. The team went through their various exercises and, as they were making their way up the beach, they ran into Rocco's team.

Ace came over to him. "Hey, how's everything going?"

"It's going," Bird said with a wry smile.

"Listen, Piper wanted me to ask if Imogene wanted to meet up for a coffee. She knows your daughter is young but the girls enjoy playing with John and would like to meet your girl too. I know we talked about getting together, but Piper mentioned it again this morning."

The offer from Ace and Piper was more than generous and, after all he and his wife had done to prepare his house for their return, he knew Imogene would love the opportunity to meet Piper. Thank her for all the thoughtful touches she'd put into Layla's room. It would also be good for Imogene to have someone to talk to about being married to a SEAL. His wife hadn't had that opportunity before and he should've tried a little harder to understand her concerns instead of disregarding them like he had.

"I'll talk to her, but I think she'll like the idea a lot. I'll get back to you," Bird finally said.

"Sounds good." Ace clapped him on the shoulder. "See ya around."

He sprinted up the sand to catch up with his teammates and, once he got there, he headed for his pile of clothes.

"Everything okay with Ace?"

Bird looked over his shoulder and spied Fort behind him. "Yeah, he was just asking if I thought Imogene wanted to meet up with Piper for a coffee. Get to know her and all."

Fort nodded. "Probably a good idea. Do you think she'll go?"

Bird grabbed his towel to wipe the sweat and seawater off his face. "I think she will. Piper was a big help in setting up Layla's room and I know Immy will want to thank her."

Fort's eyebrows rose at his use of his nickname for his wife, but he didn't comment. "You done anything about a paternity test yet?"

Bird hadn't thought more on getting a test done. With every passing moment he spent with Layla, he didn't need a piece of paper to confirm what his mind and heart already knew—she was his. "Not yet. We were kind of busy yesterday. And well…"

"You don't need it," Fort responded with a wry grin.

Bird shrugged. "Yeah, I can't explain it. The second I saw her, I instinctively knew she was mine. You probably think I'm crazy."

"No, I just don't want to see you go down the dark path you went when Imogene left you. You almost seemed on a suicide mission back then."

Bird didn't need to be reminded of that time and how he'd walked the fine line of putting him and his team at risk. He was lucky the guys hadn't lobbied to have him booted out. "Thanks, Fort, but it's different this time."

Fort studied him and, if he wanted to say anything more, he swallowed his words. "Okay, but know we've always got your back."

"Thanks, means a lot. I'll see you on base." He lifted his hand and walked away from his team lead and the rest of the guys who'd been standing off to one side while he and Fort talked. They would've heard the conversation and he could see skepticism in their eyes.

Did they not believe he had it together this time?

He'd fought side by side with that group of men. They'd endured hell, being held captive for a couple of weeks. They were more than teammates, they were brothers-in-arms. Yet, right at that moment, Bird felt more disconnected from them than he had when he'd first joined the team.

None of them had kids. They couldn't understand the way he had intrinsically known Layla was his daughter the second he held her in his arms. The way she trusted him to keep her safe when she placed her hand in his. Until they had their own children, they wouldn't understand that bond.

What hurt him the most was that his team lead didn't trust his instincts. The same instincts that they all relied on when they were on a mission. Nobody questioned anyone when they said their instincts were screaming danger was just around the corner. They believed and trusted their teammate to be right. And they always were.

So why didn't they trust him this time?

* * *

Bird PULLED up into the driveway and shut the engine off. The front door opened and Imogene and Layla appeared. All the disappointment about his team's lack of faith in him disappeared and he was out of the car, striding to where they stood.

"Hey, here are my girls." He wrapped his arms around them, not caring that fine sand and salt, mingled with sweat, coated him. He needed this connection with his family.

"Oh, you stink," Imogene exclaimed as she pulled out of his embrace. "I'd forgotten that."

"Didn't seem to bother you yesterday."

She shrugged. "Maybe you worked out harder today than you did yesterday."

Bird laughed and pressed a quick kiss on her lips and on Layla's head. "I'll have you know I work hard every day at PT."

"Sure you do."

He shook his head at their light-hearted banter. He loved that she felt so comfortable being back with him that they could joke around like they were. "Let me shower and then we can go get something to eat."

"Not needed. I've made breakfast."

"You did?"

"You seem surprised."

"No, it's not that, it's just I'm surprised we've got any food in the fridge. We didn't get to the store yesterday."

"Well, we do, because you know Layla and I had lunch yesterday." She shrugged and hitched Layla a little higher on her hip. Their daughter was clutching a toy as she looked between the two of them, her brow furrowed.

He reached out and brushed his thumb over the

crease. "Hey princess, Daddy's sorry for sounding grumpy to Mommy."

Layla ducked her head against Imogene's neck and his stomach dropped at the thought that he might have lost some of the trust he'd had with her. Every other morning, she'd been happy to see him.

"Don't be offended. She woke up grumpy today." Imogene stepped back into the house. "Come on, the food's gonna get cold."

Bird followed his family inside, his heart warming when Layla lifted her head from the safety of Imogene's shoulder and smiled. All was right in his world.

The aroma of bacon and sausage assailed his senses the closer he got to the kitchen. His stomach grumbling appreciatively.

"You remembered," he commented when he sat down and saw the plates of food on the table.

"Again, you sound surprised. We were married for five years, Leighton. I recall most of your habits." As she put Layla in her high chair, Imogene kept her head down, so he couldn't see her expression. But she couldn't hide the hurt in her voice.

Moving quietly, he was at her side when she straightened and turned. He wrapped his arms around her. "I'm sorry, Immy. I'm saying all the wrong things." He lowered his head until their lips were almost touching. "I remember everything too."

Bird closed the distance and pressed his lips against hers. Imogene remained stiff in his arms and he thought she was going to push him away. A second later her muscles relaxed and relief swept through him. He would never get tired of kissing her. Knowing that she was within arm's reach now, not living somewhere he didn't know, settled his soul.

The shorts he wore did nothing to hide his arousal from her and she ground her hips against him. He found the hem of her shirt and pushed it up, trailing his hands up her back, underneath the fabric. He wanted to rip it off and feast on her breasts. Sit her on the kitchen counter and sample the delectable treats that lay beneath her clothes.

He began to move them toward the counter, but her hands clenched his T-shirt.

"Layla," she murmured against his lips and pulled away from him. He didn't quite relinquish his hold on her. He needed to hold her for just a few more seconds.

"Damn, I didn't think."

She chuckled and walked over to the sink, her hands gripping the edges, her spine erect as if she was trying to stop herself from wanting what he wanted—him deep inside of her. "There's three of us now. We don't quite have the freedom we once had." She straightened and faced him. Her lips were plump from his kisses and there was a rosy glow to her cheeks. "Sit. Eat. I know you need to get to base soon."

Real life came crashing down on him. The last thing he wanted to do was leave his family, but he loved knowing that, at the end of the day, he was no longer coming home to an empty house. He was coming home to his wife and daughter.

Layla slapped her hand on the plastic tray of her chair. "Eggs, Mommy?"

Imogene went to get Layla's plate but Bird held up his hand. "Let me, please?"

She nodded and he picked up the plate resting on the table in front of Layla. He put some scrambled eggs on it along with a slice of bacon and a sausage. He paused for a moment before placing it in front of his daughter. He had no idea if she liked bacon and sausage. She'd only said eggs.

He sat down with a plop, the plate still in his hand as realization suck in—he really didn't know anything about what his daughter liked and disliked. Bird looked up at Imogene. "She asked for eggs but does she like this?"

Imogene's face softened and she came over to him, cupping his cheek. He loved that she was feeling comfortable enough to touch him so freely. "Yeah, babe, she does. There's not much our little girl doesn't like to eat."

A lump lodged in his throat. There was so much he needed to learn about being a dad, but he would learn it all. There was nothing he wouldn't do for his daughter.

Or his wife.

CHAPTER 10

IMOGENE GAZED OUT THE WINDOW AS THE SUN BEGAN TO dip below the horizon. Leighton had called to say that he was going to be stuck at work for a couple more hours. They were going over some intel they'd received. He told her to go ahead and eat and he'd call when he was heading home.

She sighed and turned her back on the scene. Layla was lying on her little couch, watching one of her favorite animated movies. It was white noise to Imogene. Layla had watched it so many times that Imogene could quote it if she so desired. Once it was finished, she'd put Layla to bed.

A mixture of sadness and relief had flowed through her when they'd sat down to eat their dinner. Sadness because Layla hadn't asked where Leighton was, and relief for the same reason. They hadn't been together long enough to establish a routine where it was the three of them at dinner on a regular basis. So her young daughter wasn't used to having something and then not having it.

Of course, eating by themselves was going to happen more than just this night. If they were looking over intel, it meant that a mission was in the cards soon.

Imogene closed her eyes and concentrated on her breathing, trying to keep the panic at bay. They'd only just started on their journey to being a family and Leighton could go away soon.

How long would it be for this time?

She hadn't even asked about that mission, his last one had gone on for so long she'd been afraid that she'd never see him again. Those abandonment thoughts and her pregnancy hormones had made her so crazy with worry that she'd acted impulsively and walked away.

This time when he went, she couldn't do that. It wasn't just her anymore. And after watching father and daughter together at breakfast this morning, and seeing how their relationship was beginning to develop, she wouldn't do anything to jeopardize that.

"Mama, sit wif me." Lost in her thoughts, she hadn't noticed Layla had toddled over to her and was now clutching her pant leg. Eyes the same as her father's looked up at her and the little girl's smile melted away Imogene's fears and worries.

"Sure, sweetheart, let's go sit on the couch." The second she sat down, Layla clambered up and snuggled into her lap. Imogene breathed in the lavender scent of the soap she'd used in Layla's bath. The fragrance soothed her daughter so that falling asleep was no longer was a battle.

"Where Daddy?"

Imogene smoothed a hand over her baby fine hair. "He's at work. He'll be home soon." How many times would she have to tell her little girl the same words during her lifetime?

Layla yawned and her eyelids drooped. This was something she'd never get tired of, her daughter falling asleep in her arms. Imogene adjusted the way she was sitting so that Layla was in a more comfortable position and cherished the moment. She was well aware that the older her daughter got, the less she'd do this. Already Layla was displaying an independent streak similar to that of her father. More and more of Leighton's genes were shining through and she wondered if Layla had gotten anything from her.

The shrill of her cell phone penetrated the air. It was in the kitchen and the last thing she wanted to do was disturb Layla, but it could be Leighton calling and she didn't want to miss it. Carefully, she scooted to the edge of the couch, twisting to place Layla gently on the cushions. Even as she was making sure the little girl wouldn't fall, she was aware that the call would go to voicemail. She'd have to let Leighton know that sometimes she couldn't just pick up the phone quickly. Or, alternatively, she could make sure the phone was within reach at all times. A new habit she should get into.

The call ended the second she picked up her device. Looking at the screen she saw the missed call came from a blocked number. Her stomach pitched as she remembered the call she'd received that morning. She hadn't had the chance to tell Leighton about it because of the kiss they'd shared, the way he'd lingered way too long with the two of them over breakfast, and the rush for him to get out the door and back to base.

It wasn't something she'd wanted to mention over the

phone either. Each time Leighton had called during the day, she hadn't even given it a second thought. Pleasure that he called regularly while he was busy had thrummed through her.

She jumped when the device began ringing again. This time it was Leighton's name flashing on her screen. Imogene quickly connected the call. "Hey, are you on your way home?"

"Yeah," he sighed and she imagined his head was resting against the headrest of his car. "I'll be home in about fifteen minutes."

"Okay, dinner is waiting for you."

"I suppose it's too much to ask that Layla is still awake?"

She chuckled softly. "Yeah, babe, sorry. She fell asleep a little while ago."

"Damn. I thought as much, but I was hoping."

Over the line she could hear the disappointment in his voice. Ever since he'd laid eyes on his daughter, he'd taken his fatherly duties seriously. The action shouldn't have surprised her. Her husband was a man who committed with his whole being to any task thrown at him or anything he set his mind to.

"It's okay. She fell asleep in my arms, so when you get home, you can pick her up and tuck her in."

"You're on. See ya soon, Immy."

"Bye." The call ended and she hugged herself, keeping the joy of having her husband back close to her.

Her phone shrilled again and she swiped the call without looking at the screen. "The more you call, the longer it will be before you get home." Silence greeted her response and her smile died on her lips. Apprehension splintered over her skin like a crack in a windshield. "Who is this?"

"You made a big mistake, you know." A tinny voice sounded in her ear.

"What are you talking about? What mistake?" Her mind was screaming at her to cut the call. To not engage but, like driving past a car wreck and needing to see what happened, she couldn't make herself disconnect the call.

"You could've had it all. You could've had the perfect life. Instead, you left. But don't get too comfortable. Because if I can't have you, no one can."

The call ended and the phone slipped through her numb fingers and clattered on the counter. She didn't register the sound. Her mind whirled with what the person said to her. She couldn't tell if the caller was male or female, because the voice had been distorted. Immediately, she crossed off the possibility that it was a woman who'd been calling her. Yes, she had female friends in San Antonio, but not once had she ever picked up that one of them liked her in the way the caller suggested. And, apart from Brent, she hadn't had too many males in her life. As much as Brent seemed upset with her for leaving with Leighton, she still couldn't imagine he'd hurt her.

Or was she just being too trusting?

A hand landed on her shoulder and she yelped in fright, jumping away from the touch.

"Shit, Immy, it's me. I'm sorry I scared you. I said your name a couple of times. I thought you heard me."

The second it sank in that the person touching her was Leighton and not the creep who'd called her, she rushed to him and clamped her arms tightly around his waist. His familiar warmth and scent cascaded over her when his arms banded around her.

She didn't know how long they stood like that, but the steady *thump thump* of his heartbeat sounding in her ear slowed her own heart and tempered the fear that had consumed her after the call.

As if sensing her calming her down, Leighton pulled away and lifted her chin with his finger. "What the fuck is going on? Are you hurt? Where's Layla? Is she okay?"

Fear for her daughter sprang to life and she rushed to the living room. She fell to her knees by the couch and cupped her daughter's cheek, the warm flesh a welcome feeling. "She's okay."

"Imogene, you'd better tell me why the hell you freaked out when I got home and mentioned our daughter. Or I'm going to lose my shit."

She stood on shaky legs and faced her husband, her hand covering her mouth. Standing before her wasn't her affable husband, but the Navy SEAL he was. His lips were compressed in a thin line. His brow was furrowed. He looked fierce and commanding and sexy, all at the same time. "I'll tell you everything, but we need to put Layla to bed."

His eyes narrowed in frustration, but then he glanced over at Layla and his face softened. "Okay, but don't think you're going to get away with not saying anything. This is too important to disregard. You're both too important."

"I know, you have my word."

He nodded and then strode over to the couch, scooping up Layla without any effort. He disappeared down the hall to her room. She should follow him, but she needed a few minutes to get her composure. The call had thrown her, and she didn't know who it was or why she was being targeted. She had kept mostly to herself while she'd been living in San Antonio. As far as she could remember, she hadn't upset or offended any of the people she'd associated with.

Needing reassurance that her family was safe, she headed toward Layla's room, stopping when she spied Leighton squatting by the crib, his hand through the wooden slats, holding onto Layla's hand. His eyes were shut, but his lips moved, as if he were saying a silent prayer. Not wanting to disturb the moment between father and daughter, she backed up and returned to the living room. After checking that the windows were locked, she perched herself on the edge of the couch.

A few moments later Leighton walked back into the room. She hopped up from where she was seated. "Let me get you your dinner. I have it warming in the oven. I hope it hasn't dried out too much."

Ducking past him, she escaped to the kitchen and pulled the plate out of the oven. She set it on the counter and then rested her hands on the cool quartz.

"Talk to me, Immy, and tell me what's going on," Leighton spoke softly behind her. She wanted nothing more than to sink into his arms and have him kiss her so that she could avoid talking about the phone call she'd received.

Why was she being so afraid to talk to her husband? The man faced down terrorists and God knows who or what else every time he went on a mission. If anyone could protect her, it would be the man standing behind her. But there was still so much to sort out. They'd placed a Band-Aid over their relationship. They hadn't really talked about her leaving and what he'd done in the interim.

God, she didn't even know if he'd taken up with another woman. The thought of anyone but Leighton touching her had been abhorrent. But could the same be said for him?

She had to learn to trust him again. She was a stronger person than she'd been when they'd first gotten married. She had to be, being a single mother and all.

Turning, she placed her hands on his chest. "I'll explain everything while you eat."

* * *

BIRD SHOVELED another forkful of food in his mouth, not tasting the burst of flavors from the curry Imogene had made. She sat across the table from him, her fingers clenched together in front of her.

The lost look on her face had frightened him when he'd walked in after work. He hadn't exactly been quiet, and he'd expected her to admonish him for making so much noise he could've woken Layla. Instead she'd stared blankly at the wall, seeming to not hear him when he called her name a few times.

The look of abject fear in her eyes when she turned to face him after he touched her had adrenaline flowing through him. He wanted to find out who'd put that look on her face and tear them apart. It was apparent she didn't want to start the conversation between them. That had been the downfall for the both of them when they'd first been married. They hadn't talked enough. He was going to keep the lines of communication open this time because there was no way he was going to mess up this second chance with his wife.

As much as he wanted to find out what had happened to her prior to him walking in, they also needed to talk about the past.

If she wasn't going to start the conversation, then it was up to him.

"When I came home from my mission and found you gone, I sat down in the middle of the room, your note in my hand, for a good twelve hours. I couldn't believe you'd left me. The guys were ringing me but I didn't even hear their calls. Fort pounded on the front door for at least ten minutes before I heard it and finally answered."

She gasped and he looked up, the tears welling in her eyes struck him in the heart. "I'm so sorry, Leighton," she whispered. "You don't know how sorry I am to have caused you so much pain."

He pushed the half-empty plate aside, his appetite gone. Standing, he reached across the table and picked up her hand. "Come on, let's sit where it's more comfortable."

Imogene rose and her fingers squeezed his as he led her to the living room. Once they were seated, he continued. "I understand now why you thought you needed to leave. Where you were emotionally and mentally. Do I wish it were different? Hell yes, but I have to accept it; otherwise, it's going to eat away at us and I don't want that. I know I'd been gone a lot longer than I thought I would for that mission. Everything that could go wrong on it did. But you also know that's part of my job. I can't tell you where I'm going or how long I'm going to be gone."

He closed his eyes and rested his head against the back

of the couch. If this was an issue Imogene wouldn't be able to get over, then there really was no hope for them. He supposed he could give up being a Navy SEAL and go into private security, but a little part of him would die. He would worry that he would end up resenting her for the decision.

Dammit, now he was sounding selfish. There had to be a way they could reach a compromise.

"Babe." Her fingers brushed his forehead and he opened his eyes to gaze into her gray ones. "I'm a different person now, compared to who I was then. It's taken awhile and a lot of therapy, but I'm mentally stronger now than I was back then. It started with needing to be there for our daughter. I should've made more of an effort to find you. To tell you about Layla. That will always be something I can't change. I understand your job is who you are. How important it is to you and how it makes you the man you are sitting next to me. I can't ask you to leave something you love."

"I would if you'd asked me to." Contrary to his thoughts only seconds ago, he would leave the Navy if that's what Imogene wanted. He loved her and would do anything to make her happy. He also had Layla to think about too. Love for his family was worth the sacrifice he'd make to his career.

"I know you would, but you don't have to, because I'm not going to ask you to do it. I can handle you going away, I promise."

"Even if the mission is extended like last time, and you don't know where I am or can't get any information out of the base?"

"Yes, even then. I can't deny I won't be afraid and

worry that something may happen to you. But I won't let it cripple me. I can't. I have Layla, I have to be strong for her. And I have to be strong for you. You need to know that when you leave, I've got everything under control here on the home front. You don't need that extra worry, not when your life and the lives of your teammates are on the line."

Momentary doubts flitted through his mind, worry that Imogene was just saying the words to appease him. He studied her face. Her grey eyes shone bright and there was no hint of fear in them. Her chin lifted as if she was aware of the uncertainty flowing through him.

"We're a team, Leighton. Now you're back in my life, I don't ever want you out of it."

Bird picked up their joined hands and brushed his lips across her knuckles. "I don't want you out of my life either." What he was about to say was going to be hard but she needed to know what happened to him and his team on that mission. "What I'm about to tell you is going to be hard to hear, but it needs to be said. Are you open to listening?"

Her chest rose and fell, and her fingers clenched his briefly. "Yes. Yes, I am." She spoke with conviction and he believed she'd be able to handle what he was about to tell her.

"I can't give you specifics of where we were or what we were doing, but the mission was a disaster from the second we landed. Everything that could go wrong did. We ended up getting captured."

She gasped. Her response wasn't unexpected, but he wouldn't sugarcoat it for her. Everything had to be laid out on the table if they were going to move forward.

"They separated us and I had no idea where my team-mates were or what condition they were in. The rebels were relentless in their beatings. All I could think about was you and how I'd let you down."

"Oh God, don't ever think that. You've never let me down."

"Haven't I?" he asked, gazing at the black screen of the television. "I should've seen that you weren't coping well with my change in career. I should've seen the fears from your childhood were taking over. I should've paid more attention and made more of an effort to talk to you about what I was feeling and thinking."

Her fingers pressed against his lips. "And I should've done the same. I should've been up front with you about my thoughts and where they were taking me. Don't take the blame when it's not your burden to bear. I was the one who walked out."

Bird studied her again, looking over her features. Like before, her eyes were clear. The sincerity and trust and... was that love?...blazing out of her gave him is answer. "We both made mistakes, but they're in the past. We learn and move forward."

Her hands framed his face and he lifted his own to keep them trapped against him. "Yes. Yes, we move forward. Together, Leighton."

"Together," he whispered and threaded his fingers through her hair. He closed the gap and kissed her. Their lips met in a soft touch. A touch full of promise and forgiveness. Desire burned low in his belly and, as much as he wanted to let it run free and consume him, he wasn't going to stop the most honest conversation they'd shared in their relationship.

They broke the kiss and stared at each other for endless seconds before Imogene spoke. "Tell me how you got free."

Reliving the dark days of that mission was hard, but it was important to their future, so he couldn't stop now. "I'm not sure how many days we were held captive. I'd been trying to free myself from the chains that bound my wrists and feet, but they were tight and I didn't have a lot of maneuverability. Somehow, Cricket found a piece of wire around where they held him captive. Not sure how he managed it, but he was able to get his chains undone and then he freed Fort. Between the two of them, they found our packs and weapons. Together, they took out the rebels who held us, and then they located me and the other guys."

He shook his head in remembrance of that time. How the sound of gunfire had jolted him awake and he'd waited for whoever was shooting to come in and kill him. His last thoughts had been of Imogene and her beautiful smile. But he wasn't going to tell her about that. Some things were better left unsaid. "The guys who held us, while they were strong and had some mean punches, they weren't very bright. Leaving our packs and weapons around made it so much easier for Cricket and Fort to take control of them.

"Once we were all free, we hoofed it out of there and found our way to the extraction site we'd agreed on at the start of the mission. Fort contacted the commander using the satellite phone the kidnappers hadn't taken, and we got airlifted out. We all spent a couple days in hospital at the German base getting our injuries attended to. I ended up with a couple of cracked ribs and a broken wrist. As well as cuts and bruises. None of the guys were badly injured but we needed some shots to counteract any infection we may have gotten. When we finally landed at base, I could've kissed the ground. It was so good to be back. We did our debrief and then I came home."

"To me…gone."

"Yeah to you, gone. As I said, I sat on the floor with your note in my hand in a state of shock."

"Shit, babe, I'm so sorry. So sorry that I caused you so much pain." The tears tracked down Imogene's face and his heart clenched at her loud sobs. He pulled her close and let her cry, circling her back in soothing motions.

When her sobs turned to hiccups, he spoke quietly. "That's all in the past now. We can't keep going back over it. It's time to move forward."

"Yes." Imogene snuggled up into his side and he held her tightly, grateful for the twist of fate that put him in San Antonio at the right place and the right time. They sat like that for a few minutes, not saying anything, just reveling in the fact that they were together.

Bird would've liked nothing more than to scoop her up and take her to bed. Ravish her body to cement the commitment they'd made to each other again. But there was still more they needed to discuss.

"What happened tonight, Immy? What caused you to look so frightened when I got home?"

A shudder rippled through her and he sat a little straighter, adjusting her so that she was comfortable. Her fingers played with the buttons on his shirt, almost like she didn't want to look him in the face.

"Whatever you say, I'm not going to judge you. You have to believe that."

"I know. It's just that I'm not sure what to make of a call I received. Whether I'm making more out of it than I need to."

"Nothing should ever be dismissed, no matter how small. Tell me about the call. Who was it from?"

"I don't know. The number was blocked."

His muscles tensed and he willed them to relax. The last thing she needed was to feel his tension when she was scared herself. "What about the caller? Male or female? Did you recognize the voice?"

She shook her head. "They used something to distort their voice. I think it was male, but I could be wrong. The tenor seemed low, so unless a woman was using the device and lowering her voice to make it unrecognizable, then it would have to be male." Imogene looked away from him and he waited. There was more she wasn't telling him. He could wait. He didn't have anywhere he needed to go.

Eventually she raised her gaze to his. "I got another call earlier today too."

Fuck.

CHAPTER 11

ANGER SHONE IN LEIGHTON'S GAZE, TURNING HIS normally bright-green eyes dark, like a dense forest. His lips were compressed together so tightly there was a ring of white around his mouth.

"You had another call today and you didn't tell me about it?" His voice was low and gravelly and scraped along her spine. "When did that happen?"

She sighed. "This morning while you were at PT. I was going to tell you when you got home but…"

Leighton sat back and rolled his shoulders. At least he was trying to relax himself. "Can I have your phone, please?"

Imogene pushed away from the couch and got her phone. She held it out to him, but didn't release it straightaway. "I don't think you're going to be able to find anything. The number was blocked."

"Do you trust me?" he asked.

That was a loaded question if there ever was one. But

at the end of the day, the answer was easy for her. "Unequivocally, yes. I trust you, Leighton."

"I will do everything I can to find out who called you. I know a guy, Tex, he's a tech wizard. He can find anyone and anything."

"Why didn't you ask him to find me?" The words burst out of her and she hadn't even consciously thought them. What would she have done if Leighton had turned up on her doorstep? Probably exactly what she did when he turned up at that picnic—return to him.

From the moment they met, there had been an invisible thread between the two of them. No matter how many times she'd thought she'd cut it when she'd left him two years ago, she hadn't really. Every day she hoped he'd turn up, demanding she return home to him. But when she'd gone to find him and found out that he'd moved from the very house they were now living back in, she'd taken off her blinkers and reality had set in. He hadn't cared for her as much as she cared for him. Or so she thought. Because he had kept the house and he'd made sure that her and Layla's homecoming was sweet and memorable.

Leighton's shoulders drooped and the anger seemed to fade away from his face. "I should've. I thought about it many times, but then I stopped myself."

Imogene sat down again. The truth was beginning to come out. This was the talk they need to have to be able to move forward. "Why did you stop yourself?"

He closed his eyes and pinched the bridge of his nose. She clenched her fists to keep herself from reaching out and grabbing his hand. Holding it tight and letting him know that it didn't matter now, because they were together and that's all that was important. Yet, she couldn't, because she needed to know why he hadn't come looking for her.

"I didn't want to find out that you'd moved on. That you didn't need or want me anymore." He looked at her, desolation made his green eyes murky. Lines she hadn't seen before were etched on either side of his mouth. He reached beneath his shirt and pulled out a chain. Hanging from the end of it was the wedding band she'd given him. Since they'd gotten back together, she hadn't noticed that he wasn't wearing his ring. Then again he'd always taken it off when he'd gone on a mission, leaving it in the box it had come in, in his T-shirt drawer. Her own engagement and wedding ring were tucked away in her underwear drawer. He hadn't asked about why she wasn't wearing them and she hadn't said anything either.

His fingers stroked the gold band as if it was his most-prized possession. "I've kept this close to my heart the whole time we've been apart, even when I've gone on missions. I had hope that one day you'd come back. I just never expected when I saw you again, we'd have a daughter."

Guilt and regret slammed into her with the force of a wave knocking her off her feet. She got off her chair and crouched beside him. "I'll keep saying it, but it's true—I'm sorry. I should've done more to get in touch with you when I was mentally better. I shouldn't have let the fact that you weren't living here give me an easy out from telling you about Layla."

Leighton hauled her up and onto his lap. Instinctively, she wrapped her arms around his neck. "No. You're not to blame. We both are, if you really want to apportion blame.

I could've made more of an effort to find you. It works both way, Immy. But we're together now and we have to make sure that we don't let anything like that happen again. And the first step was you telling me about the calls you received. You could've ignored it and played it off as inconsequential, but you didn't."

Leighton's reminder of those calls turned her blood cold again. "I couldn't keep them from you. It wouldn't be right. There's Layla to think about now."

"I'll get in touch with my guy, Tex. Give him your phone number and he'll work his magic and see if he can trace the origins of the call." He pressed a kiss on her lips and she melted against him. She was sure he only meant the kiss to be a reassuring one, but like always, passion flared to life between them.

The couch creaked and she clung a little tighter to him when it became obvious that he was lifting her. They kissed the whole way to the bedroom and the second they were in the room, he placed her gently on the bed, pulling his lips away from hers. "I promise I will do everything in my power to keep you and Layla safe."

The intensity of his gaze cemented the vow he was making. "I know, babe. I know."

* * *

BIRD GAZED down at the woman in his arms. Their love-making had been intense, as if they were worried that someone would come and tear them apart again. He really wanted to ask her if there was anyone in San Antonio who could be behind the calls. He hadn't meant for the kiss to lead them to the bedroom, but he wasn't sorry it did. The threat of him leaving soon was hanging over him. He needed to let her know that Ace asked if she'd like to meet up with Piper. That meeting should take place before he went away…that is, if Immy was keen on the idea.

She stirred and he tightened his hold on her. Right here in his arms was where she belonged, not thousands of miles away.

"Babe? Everything okay?" His cock twitched at the sound of her sleepy voice.

"Yeah, go back to sleep. I've got you."

She shifted and the sheet covering her slipped down, exposing her breast. He didn't think she was even aware of what her action had caused. "Something's troubling you, I can tell. Talk to me. Didn't you say a few hours ago that we needed to make sure we talked."

"It's two in the morning, not the most ideal time to have a deep conversation."

"Your thoughts are keeping you awake, so we might as well talk about them. Might make it easier for you to sleep."

"I don't want to upset you again by telling you what I'm thinking."

"And you think by not saying anything, it's going to be better? Don't shut me out again. Tell me what's going on. What's troubling you so much that you're awake instead of sleeping?"

As much as he didn't want to agree, she had a point. He'd been the one to say that they had to make every effort possible to keep the lines of communication open between them. "There are two things I was thinking about. One good and one not so good."

117

"Well, I'm pretty sure the not-so-good thing you're thinking about are the phone calls. What's the good thing?"

As much as leading with the good appealed to him, it was probably better that he finish off with that and start off with the bad. "I'll leave the good till we've talked about the not-so-good."

"I'd prefer the good, but maybe you're right. We should leave it until we've got the bad out of the way."

"Yep."

Her husky laugh echoed around the room, setting his desire from slow burn to hot burn. The temptation to forget all about talking was strong, but he pressed it down. Afterward, when they were all talked out, he'd show her again how much he loved her.

"You're right," he started. "I was thinking about the calls and whether there was anyone in San Antonio that could be responsible for them. Is that a possibility? Was there someone you were seeing before I turned up?" It practically killed him to say that, but he had to ask.

"No. I haven't looked at another man since a certain sailor caught my eye in the grocery store more than seven years ago."

He appreciated her attempt at lightening the mood. "I need to meet this guy."

She punched him lightly on his bicep. "Seriously, though, Layla has been my focus. Dating was so far down on my list of things to do, it wouldn't see the light of day for years."

Her declaration made him want to pound his chest like a caveman. Knowing that she hadn't desired anyone else, filled him with joy. Such an arrogant response, but he couldn't change the emotions Imogene elicited inside of him. "Same for me. I haven't needed anyone but you since that day."

She pressed a soft kiss right over his heart and, when she settled herself against his side, he placed his palm over the spot, imprinting her kiss on his heart. "The only person I talked to regularly was my neighbor, Brent, but that was only general chit chat. He never showed any interest in me."

Bird sat up straighter, dislodging Imogene from his chest. "Wait…that was the guy from the picnic, right? The one who didn't seem happy to see you leaving with me. The one who always sent death-ray looks in my direction whenever I turned up at your place before you came back with me."

Why the fuck hadn't he thought of this guy the second Imogene told him about the phone calls? It was so obvious he was the one calling her.

"No, Brent wouldn't make calls like that. I don't believe it."

"Immy, in most cases when it comes to kidnapping, stalkers, and other weird shit, it's usually someone you know. The guy gave me creep vibes the second I met him."

Her fingers drew circles on his chest and the touch had his cock standing to attention. "I'm not sure. He wouldn't block his number to me."

"Do you know his number? Is it in your phone?" A shaft of jealousy deflated his ardor at the thought of Imogene's loser neighbor being listed in her contacts.

"Yes, I have his number."

Bird couldn't help the growl from escaping him.

"Control your alpha instincts, would you? I had

Brent's number so that if I heard something during the night that freaked me out, I could call him and he could check it out. He was being neighborly."

If that asshole had given her his number to be a good neighbor, Bird would eat his combat boots. He may have phrased getting Imogene's number and she getting his that way, but Brent was a guy, and guys always had ulterior motives. He should know. He'd made it impossible for Imogene to leave the grocery store the day they'd met without getting her number and giving his to her.

Another punch landed on his bicep, only harder. "Ouch," he said, rubbing the spot she hit.

"Pfft, that probably didn't even register. But I'm serious...there's no way Brent would hurt me or Layla. He's got a son and daughter of his own. He would protect them with his life."

"Does he have custody of them?"

"No, he has shared custody with his wife. His kids were with him at the picnic that weekend."

"Still, I'll tell Tex about him and, if he's not involved, I'll let you say *I told you so*."

"I can get on board with that."

"Is there anyone else? What about other moms or people you worked with."

"Most of the moms I know are too busy with their own kids to threaten me and worry about what I was doing in my private life. The two girls I worked with, Trixie and Carol, wouldn't hurt a fly. So, no, I don't think it's any of them. Maybe it's a wrong number."

"I doubt it's a wrong-number scenario."

"That's what I'm going to put out into the universe. How about you tell me the good now?"

"Piper, the woman who helped with setting up Layla's room and organized the designer, wants to meet up with you."

Her body tensed beneath his fingers, but then a breath shuddered out and her muscles relaxed. "I'd like to be able to thank her for all she did for us."

"Good. I'll put her number in your phone and you can call when you're ready. But don't leave it too long, okay?" The sooner Imogene started to get friendly with some of the other women around base, the easier it would be for her to deal with his absences.

"That's fine." Her hand trailed down his chest, sliding beneath the sheet. His breath hitched when her fingers closed around his hard length. "So I'm awake now and I can see you aren't tired. What shall we do?"

Bird pushed her hair away from the side of her face. "I don't know. What did you have in mind?"

Her lips stretched into a wicked smile. "How about I surprise you?"

"I don't normally like surprises but I'm okay with you giving them to me."

"Good," she said as she slid down, and her mouth replaced her hands. His hips jerked when her tongue swirled around the tip of his cock and her hand squeezed his balls.

"Immy. So good." He closed his eyes and let his wife use her wicked mouth and tongue on him. Her hand followed her mouth up and down creating an amazing friction. He wasn't going to last long and, as much as he wanted to come inside of her mouth, he wanted to feel her muscles clench around him and bring him to release.

Reaching down, he lifted her, dislodging her mouth

from his cock. Her pout of dissatisfaction was the last thing he saw before his mouth crashed into hers and he rolled her so that he was on top.

He stroked down her body, tweaking her nipples before squeezing them. She bit his lip. "Hmm…you like it rough, huh?"

"No, I'm annoyed at you for spoiling my fun." The way her body was arching beneath his fingers belied that edict.

"I promise I'll make it worthwhile," he murmured and handed her the condom he'd grabbed from the side table.

"I hope so." She licked her lips and rolled the latex over him.

A second later he thrust inside of her. Their moans mingled together as their bodies found a synchronicity that only couples who were meant to be together could find. He slid a hand beneath her hips and lifted so he could deepen his penetration.

"I love you." The words burst out of him. He hadn't meant to say them but now that they were out in the world, he wasn't sorry. He'd never stopped and Immy needed to know that.

"I love you too." Her body clenched around him and she rolled her hips, as if seeking her release. He increased his pace and, two strokes later, they shattered around each other.

With their breathing slowly returning to normal, Bird changed positions so that Imogene was laying across his body.

"I mean it, Immy. I love you and I'm not letting you go."

"I don't want you to."

CHAPTER 12

Two days later, Imogene looked up as Leighton walked through the front door in the middle of day.

"Daddy!" Layla scrambled off the ground where they'd been doing some simple puzzles, zoomed across the room, and launched herself at her father.

He scooped her up and held her tightly against his chest. From where Imogene sat, she could see the fine lines of tension around his eyes. Her stomach dropped—there was only one reason Leighton was home in the middle of the day, and it wasn't because he missed them.

"You're going away, aren't you?"

Leighton looked over the top of their daughter's head and met her gaze directly on. "Yeah, the area we've been monitoring has heated up. We're wheels up in two hours."

Everything in her wanted to ask him where he was going. And how long he'd be away. But she swallowed down the questions because he couldn't answer them for her.

"Do you need me to do anything?" she asked, getting to

her feet and going over to the two loves of her life. Once she reached them, Leighton pulled her into his hug with Layla.

Layla giggled. "Mommy hug too."

"Yeah, princess, Mommy gets a hug too."

They stood there for a few moments savoring the closeness that had sprung up between them since they'd declared their love for each other. That night had cemented their reconciliation.

Layla wriggled in their arms and Imogene stepped away so that Leighton could put their daughter on the ground. The second her feet hit the tiles, she was back off to the puzzles. Leighton hauled her close. She burrowed into him and squeezed him tight.

"I'm sorry I have to go away so soon, Immy. I was hoping things would settle down and we wouldn't have to leave."

This was a big test for them and the fact it had come early in their reconciliation was something neither of them was truly prepared for. It was up to her to reassure her husband that him going away wasn't an issue with her anymore.

She put a little space between them so that he could see what she had to say. Understand that it was coming from her heart. "Leighton, I don't ever want you to apologize for having to go away. I know that you must have a million thoughts running through your mind about if I'll be here when you come back. I will be. I promise. We *both* will be here, waiting. We're not going anywhere."

A breath shuddered out of him, confirming that he'd been scared that she might flee while he was away. How many trips would it take before that wouldn't be his first thought? She didn't know, but she deserved his fear, and only had herself to blame for it. So it was up to her make it right.

"I love you, Immy," he whispered against her neck.

"Love you too, babe."

Their lips connected and their kiss was full of promise and love. As much as she wanted to drag him down to the bedroom to have him slide into her body before he left, there wasn't enough time. Plus, she didn't want to deprive her daughter of spending time with her father.

"How long will it take you to pack?" she asked.

"Not long. I've always got a pack ready for when we have to leave. I can spend a little time with both my girls. It's going to be hard to tell her I won't see her for a little bit. Will she understand?"

Imogene glanced over to where Layla had lost interest in the puzzles and was now playing with the soft princess doll Leighton had bought for her. "I don't know. She might. I imagine I'll be getting a lot of questions asking where you are. But I will deal with them. Don't you worry about us."

He reached out and cupped her cheek. "I can't help it. I still haven't heard anything from Tex after I called him about those calls you got."

Imogene had managed to push those calls out of her mind. The fact she hadn't received any since the two she'd gotten in one day had gone a long way to calming her nerves. "I'm beginning to believe that it was a case of a wrong number more than someone after me specifically. You know the only calls I've received in the last two days were from you and Piper."

"Speaking of Piper, I ran into Ace as I was leaving the

base and told him that we were shipping out. He said that if you and Layla wanted to go over to their place to spend a couple of nights, you're more than welcome."

Imogene was taken aback by the offer. "That's generous of them to offer me a place to stay, considering they've never met me."

"I don't think it matters that you haven't met Piper in person. You've talked regularly the last couple of days. She already considers you a friend."

"I don't get that," she said, shaking her head. "No one has ever considered me a friend without meeting me. I can count on one hand the number of people I've even thought of as friends."

"I know it sounds weird, but when I asked for her help to set up the house for you and Layla, she didn't even question me. Basically said that you were my wife, and that's all she needed to know."

"But I could've been a bitch. After all, I walked out on you and didn't tell you that you had a daughter."

None of this made sense to her. Her parents had never cared about her or done something as selfless as what Piper had done in setting up a house for a complete stranger.

"Immy." Leighton's hands landed on her shoulder. "Don't overthink this. You didn't have the support you needed when we were first married and that's on me. I should've made more of an effort to introduce you to the partners of some of the other SEALs. I know the guys on my team didn't keep their girlfriends for long, but there are men in other teams who have committed relationships. Now you're not alone. And it's just an offer, so you don't have to take them up on it."

Imogene took a couple of cleansing breaths, easing her anxiety. "You're right. I just need to relax and everything will be okay. Piper and I have arranged to meet up tomorrow at the park, so the kids can play."

Bird laughed. "And you didn't think to tell me this after I mentioned that Ace offered you a place to stay? And the way you reacted to the offer."

"Yeah, I probably should've. I was just shocked that they'd open their house to me."

Leighton kissed her briefly on the lips. "I'm glad you've arranged something. You don't have to stay there. It's just an idea for you to consider."

"I know." She gave him a gentle shove. "Now go spend time with your daughter."

"If you insist." He squeezed her hands again before he strode over to where Layla still sat. She spent the next few moments watching the two of them, their heads close together. The way Leighton spoke softly and gently to their daughter warmed her heart. It was in moments like this that she regretted her actions of not trying harder to get in touch with Leighton, especially when she'd come here. How hard would it have been to go to base and see if someone could get in touch with him for her? She also should've tried harder to be more involved years ago, before Layla. Then maybe she wouldn't have been so quick to let her emotions get the better of her and run away.

Or maybe it was what she needed to do. Over the time she'd been apart from Leighton, she'd grown stronger as a person. She had to, considering she had a baby to look after.

"What are you thinking about so hard?" Leighton glanced her way.

"Initially, how different things could've been if I'd tried harder. Then I worked out that maybe this was how it's meant to be. That, even though you missed so much, if we'd been together at the time, we may not have made it."

He came back and pulled her into a tight hug. "Maybe. But one thing I do know is, we can't change it. I'm glad that we're together now, that's the most important thing for me."

Imogene held him close, felt the warmth of his skin through his T-shirt, the strength of his love. She stored those sensations away, so she could bring them out whenever she needed them on the lonely nights she'd have until he returned, however many that might be. "How much more time do we have before you have to leave?"

"Five minutes."

"Oh."

"Yeah, I wish it was fifty."

She went up on tiptoe and transferred her arms from his waist to around his neck. "Then we'd better make the most of it."

"I like the way you think."

Their lips met and they slowly explored each other's mouths. Saying the things they found difficult to say. Reluctantly, Leighton pulled away and everything in her screamed at her to keep him close. But she didn't. She had to show him that she could handle him traveling.

Leighton went over again and picked up Layla. "Daddy has to go away for a while. I won't be able to talk to you on the phone but know that Daddy loves you with his whole heart. Be a good girl for Mommy."

Tears pooled in Imogene's eyes as she watched the exchange. The way Layla nodded as if she truly understood everything her daddy was saying to her.

He placed their little girl back on the ground and once again framed Imogene's face with his hands. "I love you, Immy. Don't forget that."

"I won't." She promised. "I love you too."

He swooped down for another intense kiss that was over before it had even started. He grabbed his pack and then he was out the door. Taking a piece of her with him.

* * *

THE DRONE of the aircraft's engine lulled Bird into that place where he was awake but he wasn't. The zone he and his teammates got in whenever they were on a mission and having to keep a watch.

"How's things at home?"

Bird roused and looked up to see Silver leaning on the seat in front of him.

"Good, everything's good."

"Imogene okay with you leaving?" Considering what had happened after he'd returned to find her not at home, he could understand why Silver was asking.

"Yeah, she said she was good with me leaving, and I believe her."

"I bet it's hard knowing that you're leaving your family behind."

Bird considered his teammate's words. Whenever he'd gone away in the past, he'd always been conscious that if something happened to him while on a mission, his parents and Parker would be upset, but they'd also be proud that he'd died doing something he loved while he was protecting his country. He'd always worried a little about Imogene and hoped that after a while she'd find someone else to fall in love with. Although thinking about her being with someone other than him, right now after they'd reconciled, was like the red-hot burn of a bullet ripping through his flesh. But the reality of his life was that he would hope she would move on. As for Layla, if something happened to him now, she probably wouldn't remember him. Wouldn't remember how much he loved her.

"Yeah, there's a lot more to think about now. But I want to let you know that just because I have a wife and a daughter at home, it's not going to affect my ability to do my job properly."

"I know. I'm not worried about that."

Bird was relieved his teammate felt that way. He hoped the rest of the team had the same attitude.

Silver tapped the top of the seat he was leaning against before going back to where he'd been. Bird rested his head back, wishing the flight was over. Once they landed, they'd go over the plans they'd discussed before leaving and hope like hell nothing wouldn't go wrong, causing them to get stuck for weeks on end in the shithole they were going to.

The pitch of the engines changed, indicating they had begun their descent. Bird tightened his seatbelt and made sure his pack was secure. He recalled the way Imogene had been freaking out when they'd been flying from San Antonio to Riverton. How she'd not snatched her hand away when he'd reached for it.

He hoped she and Layla were okay. He was still pissed

that Tex hadn't been able to get him any information on who had called her. Bird didn't buy Imogene's suspicions that it was a wrong number and that whoever had made those calls wasn't targeting her. He couldn't shake the feeling that danger was lurking, and here he was, a fucking million miles away from her, and couldn't protect her or Layla. He prayed that nothing would happen to his family while he was gone.

Perhaps if he put it out in the universe, it would keep his girls safe. Like Imogene had, when she said she was sure it was a wrong number.

CHAPTER 13

IMOGENE PACKED ANOTHER T-SHIRT INTO THE BAG FOR Layla. She'd taken up Piper's offer to go and spend a night with her while Leighton was away. At first she'd told the other woman it wasn't necessary when they'd met up for their play date and the kids had all gone on well. As it had been over a week since Leighton had left, she was beginning to get a little restless. A change of scenery and another woman to talk to was what she needed.

She touched her wedding and engagement rings feeling closer to Leighton. After he'd walked out the door for his mission she'd gone to her underwear drawer and put them on. Never again would she take them off.

Satisfied that she had plenty of clothes for Layla, along with her favorite toys, blanket, and books, Imogene zipped up the bag. The diaper bag was just about bursting with supplies and she planned to leave a box of diapers in the car in case she needed it. Her bag wouldn't take long to pack, since they were only spending one night, and she didn't need nearly as many things as her daughter.

As she made her way to her bedroom, her phone buzzed in her pocket. Pulling it out, she glanced at the screen. The number was blocked and immediately her heart leaped to her throat.

"It could be Leighton. Maybe he's calling me from a secure line so the number doesn't show up." Talking to herself had become a bit of a habit over the last week. It was a failed attempt at reassurance. Normally, it worked, but this time, not so much.

Swiping to accept the call she brought the device to her ear. "Hello." Static sounded down the line. Yes, it was Leighton calling. "Babe, is that you? Is everything okay?"

Another burst of static and then the line went dead. It had to be Leighton calling. When she'd received the creepy calls, both times, the person had spoken straightaway.

Her phone buzzed again and she quickly swiped it. "Leighton?" There was no static this time.

"Has he left you already?" The tinny voice echoed in her ear and she almost dropped the phone.

"Who are you? What do you want?" Her voice shook a little and she was angry at herself for letting the guy get the better of her.

"I'm the person you're supposed to be with."

"Look, I don't know who you are but you need to stop calling me." She disconnected the call. Rushing to her room, she threw her things into the bag she'd set out on the bed. Once she was happy with the items she'd packed, she collected her bag and Layla's, and rushed through the house to the kitchen where a door connected the main living area with the garage. She shoved the bags in the car and raced back inside to pick Layla up.

"Come on sweetheart, time to go see Piper and her kids. Let's get in the car."

"Yay!" Layla said and Imogene was pretty sure her enthusiasm was for the car ride and not the prospect of playing with Piper's daughters and son. Although that might change, the older she got.

Imogene sat in the driver's seat, her heart pounding, and her fingers gripped the steering wheel as if her life depended on it. She took a couple of deep breaths to get herself under control. No way could she drive this worked up.

Slowly, her breathing settled into her normal pattern and, once she was sure that she wasn't going to put herself and Layla in danger, she started the engine and opened the garage door. Looking into the rearview mirror, she couldn't see any strange cars.

Okay, she could do this. Reversing the big SUV out of the garage, she pressed the button to close it, waiting until the door shut again. The whole drive to Piper's, she constantly checked her mirrors to see if any strange cars were following her. Layla pointed out the occasional color she recognized and Imogene answered her absent-mindedly.

The second she pulled into Piper's driveway, the tension in her shoulders dissipated and she closed her eyes in relief. She'd made it.

The door to the house opened and the girls rushed out. Piper followed, holding onto John. Behind her, Layla clapped her hands in excitement. The next few minutes were a flurry of activity as she unpacked the car and got settled into the room she'd been shown to.

Piper led her to the large back deck where there was a

table set with a pitcher of iced tea and some cookies and brownies.

"This looks good, thanks Piper. You didn't have to go to this much trouble."

Her friend shrugged. "No trouble. The girls love to bake so, trust me when I say we have plenty of sweet treats, in fact, probably too many. Ace takes some to the base for the guys. They love it."

Imogene smiled at the vision of burly Navy SEALs eating a ton of cookies and brownies. "I'm pretty sure it won't go to their hips like it does with us."

"Tell me about it. But," her voiced softened as she gazed over the yard where there was a lot of squealing coming from Layla and John as the older girls tickled and chased them. "After what they endured, seeing them baking and laughing together is worth the few extra pounds."

Imogene recalled what Leighton had told her about Piper and the girls, and what he and his team had suffered in Timor Liste. "I'm not much of a baker, but I will be happy to try to learn when Layla gets a little older."

"We'll do anything for our kids, won't we?"

"We sure will."

Later that night, Imogene sat in the living room with Piper and Ace. When she'd seen him walk into the house, the first thing she had wanted to do was ask him if he knew where Leighton was and how much longer he'd be away, but she swallowed the words. Although Ace's muttered *he's fine* in her ear when he'd given her a hug suggested she hadn't been very successful in hiding her questions. She also didn't know how much truth there was to his words, because how would he know if

Leighton was okay or not? She didn't imagine there was much talking around the base of what or where the various teams were when they were on missions. But she appreciated his effort.

"What do you want to do tomorrow?" Piper asked. "We could take the kids to the beach."

"Umm, sure." The thought of being at a public beach without Leighton by her side freaked Imogene out a little and she didn't know why. She loved the beach, but Layla had only been once, and she worried that all it would take would be for her to look away for a second and something could happen to Layla in the water.

"You don't sound so keen. Sidney and Gumby have a house that backs onto the beach. It's nice and quiet and safe for the girls, if that's what you're worried about," Ace said.

Damn, the guy was observant. Why was she surprised? He was trained to read people and their actions. Leighton was that way with her, always seeing things she'd tried to hide.

"Thanks. I was a little concerned."

"We can do something else if you like," Piper responded.

"No, I think it will be fun. I love the beach and missed it when I was in San Antonio." Beside her, her phone shrilled loudly and everything in her went on high alert. After the call she had before she'd left her house, her phone had stayed ominously quiet. Picking it up from the table it had been resting on, she saw that the number was blocked. No way was she falling into that trap again. From now on, she wasn't answering her phone from a number she didn't recognize, but what if it was a number that Leighton was calling from? She didn't want to miss his calls.

Indecision rode her hard, but she hit decline and put the phone face down. Hoping against hope that she just hadn't denied Leighton's call.

"Everything okay?" asked Ace.

"Yeah, just a spam call."

"Oh God, I get so many of them. It's frustrating," Piper commiserated.

Imogene nodded and gazed out the windows at the darkness of the evening. While she was grateful that Piper had offered her a place to stay for the night, she missed being in the house she and Leighton had chosen together. But it was only for one night. She could get through this.

"Well I think I'm going to turn in." She stood and collected her phone, noting that she had voicemail. She would listen to that in the privacy of her bedroom.

"Okay, if you need anything, let us know." Piper stood as well and gave her hug. Ace watched from behind her and Imogene suspected that she hadn't fooled him one bit.

* * *

LAYLA WOKE EARLY the next morning, fussing because she wasn't in her own bed and room. While she'd slept well, Imogene was experiencing the same. There really wasn't anything like sleeping in your own bed. She still hadn't checked the voicemail. She'd meant to after she got into bed, but the second she laid down, tiredness consumed her and she'd fallen straight to sleep.

Grabbing her phone now, she unlocked it and put it to her ear to listen to the message.

Bitch, did you think you could get away from me? It's not happening. I'm go—

Imogene deleted the message, not listening to the rest of it. Why were the calls starting up again now when Leighton was away? She wished he was here so she could tell him about them.

Needing to do something constructive, she got up and got herself and Layla dressed. They headed toward the kitchen where the low murmur of conversation reached her. Walking into the large open space, Piper and the girls were already seated at the table. The aroma of something baking in the oven permeated the air. Ace was missing, but Imogene assumed he'd be at PT.

"Morning," she said brightly, hoping that Piper couldn't hear anything untoward in her voice.

"Hi, did you sleep well?"

"I did, thanks. Crashed the moment my head hit the pillow."

"That's good. Sit. I've got a breakfast casserole cooking in the oven, and it should be ready in a few minutes."

"Great." She settled Layla into the booster seat Piper had given her the previous evening and handed her daughter a couple of pieces of banana from the fruit platter in the middle of the table.

Restlessness pervaded her soul and her skin prickled with the need to keep moving. "Umm...would you mind watching Layla for about ten minutes? I need to take a walk."

Piper studied her for a few seconds. "Are you okay? Did something happen that you don't want to tell me about?"

"No, it's not that, it's just..." she shrugged, unable to

explain exactly what was happening because she didn't understand it herself. "I need some air."

"Okay." Piper didn't sound convinced that Imogene was fine, but she didn't know the woman well enough to confide in her. The way Piper talked about all the other women in the group and how well they got on, had made Imogene yearn for the same thing. She was sure Piper and her friends would welcome her into their circle. But they would always have a unique synergy that came from familiarity that Imogene wouldn't have with them—their men were teammates after all. Essentially, they were one big unit, and she and Leighton could never really be a true part of it because he had his own teammates he was close with.

"I won't be long. I'm just going to take a quick walk to clear my head."

"Don't forget your phone." Piper called as she left the kitchen.

"Okay."

Imogene rushed to her bedroom and changed out of her flip-flops into a pair of ballet flats. Not the ideal walking shoe, but they were all she had. After collecting her phone, she headed for the front door. Once outside, she took a couple of deep breaths and, when she exhaled, her mind felt a little clearer.

She headed off down the street, concentrating on her breathing, but her mind was turning over the phone calls, trying to think who could be taunting her. She didn't know who she'd offended so much that they'd wanted to come after her. Trixie and Carol, her friends from work, were fun girls, and the couple of times they'd gone out had been good evenings. When she'd quit her job, she'd told them that she was leaving because she'd reconciled with Leighton, and they'd both seemed happy for her. No way could one of them be the caller, and once this whole mess was over, she'd call them for a chat. They'd sent the occasional text since she'd moved to Riverton, but it would be more fun to speak to them.

There was also Brent who could be making the calls. Leighton definitely thought it could be him, but she still doubted that he would have any reason to want to hurt her. She hadn't done anything to encourage him into thinking there was a chance that they could have some type of future together.

Behind her, she could hear the sound of a car approaching, so she stepped a little closer to the curb to allow it to pass her safely. It slowed down and she glanced over. The window was down and her mouth dropped open when she saw who was driving the car. "What are you—?" Her words died when the person lifted a gun and pointed it directly at her.

"If you want to live, get in the car, and toss the phone in your hand."

CHAPTER 14

THE PLANE'S WHEELS BUMPED AND SCREECHED AS THEY HIT the tarmac, and the momentum of the thrust to slow the plane had Bird pressing his hand on the seat in front of him.

Home.

Excitement built in him at the thought of seeing Imogene and Layla, although that would have to wait for a few hours. They needed to debrief with the Commander about the mission they'd just completed.

"Who's up for a big juicy steak dinner once we're all finished with the debrief?" Rocket asked once the plane stopped.

There was a resounding *hell, yes* from his teammates. He would've been one of them in the past, but now not so much. "Nah, I want to get home to Imogene and Layla. I've missed them."

"Ohh, look who's under the thumb now," Hank joked.

"Fuck off. When it happens to you, you'll be the one passing up steak dinners with the team to get your woman," Bird retorted. He didn't care if the guys gave him a hard time about wanting to see his family.

The joking continued as the others took their time getting out of their seats and grabbing their packs. Bird knew exactly what they were doing and why. "You guys are assholes, you know that?"

His comments were met with laughter and he joined in too. These men were his brothers, and if it was one of the other guys who was eager to get to his woman and he was the single one, he'd be doing exactly what they were.

The second Bird stepped out of the cabin of the plane, he stopped. Standing at the bottom of the stairs was Ace, holding Layla. Commander North was at his side.

"What the fuck?" he rushed down, almost tumbling face-first onto the tarmac. "Where's Imogene?" he demanded shrugging out of his pack, letting it fall to the ground. He reached out to take Layla from Ace's arms. He closed his eyes and rested his cheek against her head, her fine hair tickling his nose.

"Sorry, Bird, Imogene went for a walk this morning and when I got home from PT, Piper was frantic with worry because she hadn't returned. She told Piper she was only going for a short walk, but she'd been gone close to an hour by the time I got home."

Terror slammed into him like a punch from the insurgents who'd held them captive all those years ago. Imogene hadn't run, had she? No, no way, she wouldn't leave Layla. His daughter whimpered in his arms and he loosened his hold on her. He pressed a kiss to her cheek. Bird was aware of his teammates coming up behind him, but he found it difficult to understand exactly what Ace was saying. "How do you know something happened to her?"

Ace reached into his pocket and pulled out Imogene's phone. The screen was smashed as if it had been dropped on the concrete. "I told Piper that maybe she'd gotten herself turned around and a little lost because she wasn't familiar with the neighborhood. I found this around the corner from our house when I went looking for her. She hadn't gone far when something happened."

"Do you think she was taken or did she run again?" Fort asked the question and, if Bird wasn't holding Layla, he would've turned and knocked his teammate to the ground.

"Don't even go there, Fort. No way would she leave Layla behind. She promised too. It's not like it was before." His anger at his team lead was immediate, but it was what his first thought had been too.

Fort held up his hands. "I had to ask."

Bird sighed and made a conscious effort to keep his anxiety under control. "I know."

"Mommy?" Layla whimpered in his arms. "Want Mommy." Then she started to cry in earnest and Bird tightened his grip on his baby girl.

"I know, princess. I know. It's going to be okay."

"Why don't we take this inside?" Commander North suggested. "Then we can sit down and strategize. You can tell us everything, Bird. I have a feeling there's something going here that you haven't told us about."

"Yes, sir," he said, as he jiggled Layla in an attempt to soothe her.

"We've got your back, Bird. We'll find her." Fort bent

and grabbed Bird's pack from where he'd dumped it so he could hold Layla.

Bird breathed out when Layla's cries settled down, knowing his team was there for him. Not that he'd ever doubted it.

They all walked into the base and headed for one of the conference rooms they normally used for strategy meetings. Walking toward them was Beck, the former SEAL who'd been a part of his team. In fact, Bird had replaced Beck when he'd gotten injured a couple of years ago. He consulted on base when he wasn't following his movie-star, actress wife, Samantha Rayse, to her film sets.

"Hey, guys, what's up?"

"Hey, Beck, good to see you." Fort gave the man a bro-hug. "Bird's wife appears to have gone missing."

"Shit, what can I do?"

Bird appreciated the offer more than he could say. He hadn't had a lot to do with Beck; after all, he'd replaced him on the team. "Any insight you may have would be appreciated," Bird responded.

When they got to the room, he found the rest of Ace's team all standing by the wall. They gave him a chin lift when he walked in. He reciprocated and sat down, making sure Layla was comfortable. His little girl's eyes were beginning to droop and he figured sleep wouldn't be far away.

Once everyone sat down, Commander North turned to Ace. "Tell us everything you know."

Ace repeated to the group what he'd told Bird when he'd stepped off the plane. Everyone listened and didn't interrupt. When he'd finished, Commander North addressed him. "Bird, do you know who may want to hurt or harm Imogene?"

"There was a day where she'd received a couple of creepy calls. A distorted voice telling her that she'd made a mistake. Before I left, she hadn't had any calls since the initial two, and she was convinced it was a wrong number."

"What did you do with this information?" North asked.

"It was a blocked number, so I contacted Tex to see if he could find out something. When I followed up with him a couple of days before shipping out, he said he hadn't been able to do too much digging. Some shit hit the fan with something he was working on, which took precedence over what I'd asked him to do."

"Do you have Imogene's number?" Beck asked. "Maybe I can contact Cass at Alliez Security, the firm Ox works for now. She's a computer whiz and may be able to get back to us sooner."

"That would be great." Bird reached into his pocket and pulled out Imogene's phone, placing it on the table. "We won't be able to ping it for her location because here it is and, with the smashed screen, I'm not sure you'll be able to do much with it."

"She probably doesn't need the physical device." Beck reached into his own pocket and pulled out his phone. After fiddling with it for a moment, he slid it across to Bird. "Give me Imogene's number and I'll give Cass a call and see what she can do."

Making sure he didn't wake up Layla, he took Beck's phone and typed in Imogene's number before handing it back. "Thanks, Beck. I appreciate it."

"Anytime. I'll leave you guys to talk and I'll call Cass. Once I hear anything, I'll come back."

Bird nodded, grateful for his help. The door shut and Commander North stood and headed for a whiteboard hanging on a wall. "Right, let's go over everything we know. Bird, are you okay there with Layla or do you want me to see if I can get someone to look after her while we talk?"

The last thing he wanted to do was relinquish his hold on his daughter. He had no plans to let her out of his sight. "I'm fine. Let's find my wife."

* * *

IN A SEEDY MOTEL ROOM, Imogene sat on the edge of the hard, wooden chair. "Carol, what's going on here?"

She'd been asking the same question over and over ever since she'd followed her instructions to get in the car. She hadn't wanted to, but she also didn't want to die and the venomous look in Carol's eyes when she'd pulled up beside her had scared her into believing the other woman would follow through with her threat.

When she'd gotten in the car, Carol had zoomed off and, ever since, she'd been muttering to herself and ignoring Imogene. Why take her if she was going to forget about her? That was another question that kept circling her mind.

Tired of being ignored, Imogene got up and strode over to where her former co-worker was standing, gazing out the window. She had no idea where the gun was. Carol had to have it on her or close by and the last thing she wanted to do was antagonize her kidnapper, but she needed answers.

How scared must Layla be? At least she was with Piper, so she wasn't alone. But her daughter had to be confused, wondering where her mommy was.

And Leighton. God, where was he? Would she ever see him again? Would Piper and Ace let Bird's commander know that something had happened to her so he could then get a message to wherever her husband was. What she wouldn't give for him to storm through that flimsy motel door and rescue her. But the likelihood of that happening was so far away, she should forget about it.

If she was going to survive, she had to save herself.

"Carol, I asked you a question. What the fuck is going on? Why are you here in California and not back in Texas?" She shouted the words in an attempt to pull her former co-worker out of the stupor she'd fallen into.

"I came for you," she said, still not looking at her.

"Why? Why did you come for me?"

"Because you need me."

Confusion swept over her. Why would Carol think she needed her? "That makes no sense. We hardly had anything to do with each other in San Antonio. I worked with you and Trixie. We went out for a couple of girls' nights but it wasn't like we were in each other's pockets."

Carol turned to face her. Malevolence shone in her kidnapper's eyes and Imogene took a step back. "That's where you're wrong, sweet Imogene. We were always together. You and me. We would go on dates. The kisses we shared were magical. We were in love, but then you left me—for a man. How could you do that?"

The woman was delusional, but Imogene was afraid of

what Carol might do if she pointed that out, if she told her that all the things she said happened between the two of them had never occurred.

Should she agree with Carol to diffuse the situation? Maybe if she calmed her down, she'd be able to find the gun, take it and then escape.

"I'm sorry."

"Sorry doesn't cut it, Imogene." Carol leaned in until her face was inches from hers. Her eyes were wide and the pupils hid most of her brown irises. "We had a future, you and I. Remember all the times we talked about it. And then you threw it all way for a goddamned penis."

Fear dug its spiky claws into her skin. With each word Carol spoke, her anger seemed to increase. There was no chance that anything she said would calm the irrational woman who'd taken her.

Imogene took two more steps back, putting space between them, and was glad to see that Carol stayed where she was. In the waistband of the woman's jeans, she spied the gun. No way was she going to be able to get it from Carol. The risk that she'd get hurt was too high. "What about Layla, Carol? I need to get back to my baby."

"Layla? Who's she? It's just you and me. Fuck, were you cheating on me with a woman and a man? What the hell, Imogene? Is everything about you a lie?"

Whatever reality Carol was living in, wasn't the one Imogene lived in. And that made her even more dangerous.

Was there a way she could get a message to another guest that she was being held against her will? A way to get a message to Piper, so maybe Ace and his team could work with the police to rescue her.

How had her life turned out like this? The last thing she'd ever imagined was a former work colleague developing a crush on her. Hell, she only worked two days a week. Sure, they'd had the occasional girls' night but not once did Carol give any indication that she was falling in love with her.

Imogene sank on the bed, rubbed her finger over her rings, and sent up a fervent prayer: *Please God, please somehow let Leighton find me.*

Was the prayer a pipe dream? Would Leighton think she'd run out on him again? No, no, he wouldn't think that. Not only were they past that, but he had to know she wouldn't leave Layla behind. Leighton *would* come looking for her, and he wouldn't stop until he found her. Of that, she was certain.

CHAPTER 15

BIRD DROPPED HIMSELF INTO A CHAIR AT THE TABLE. AFTER Ace had hounded him for the fiftieth time that Layla would be better off at his place with Piper, he'd allowed the other SEAL to take his precious daughter back to his house.

"I'm sure we'll hear something soon." Rocket came and sat next to him. "Keep the faith, man. She'll be fine."

"Thanks, and I'm trying."

"It was a good thing Ace has those cameras and we were able to see the car that kept driving past his house. If what Beck said is true about this Cass girl and her computer skills, she'll be able to trace the car as well as the origin of the calls."

"Yeah, hopefully. But is she 'Tex good?'" he countered.

"If Beck didn't think she was any good, he wouldn't have suggested her. Besides Alliez Security is an excellent firm."

"Yeah I know. I just…"

"I get it," Rocket said and drummed his fingers on the table.

Bird didn't want to think that he would never see Imogene again. Never be able to hold her or kiss her. Dammit, he'd just found her, and he couldn't lose her. Not again. Surely fate wouldn't be that cruel to him.

He pushed away from the table and began pacing around the room. He was desperate to do something. Anything. Whoever had his wife would regret that they'd taken her and they'd better not have laid a finger on her because he would break every single fucking digit on both hands.

The door burst open and Fort walked in, closely followed by Beck and Silver. Hank and Cricket had gone to get something to eat for them.

"Got her." Fort announced. He laid a tablet in the middle of the table. A woman's face filled the screen. Her dark brown hair was up in a pony tail and she wore black rimmed glasses. "Go ahead, Cass, we're all here."

"Using the footage from Ace's cameras, I was able to get a good handle on the car and a good look at the plates. I found the vehicle when I hacked into the traffic cams."

This was all well and good, but Bird just wanted to know where his wife was. "And?" he asked.

"It's a rental car. I contacted the company to ask for the information, but they weren't forthcoming, even though I asked nicely. So I did what I had to do." Even through the screen he could see she held no remorse for getting the details he needed. "The car was rented by a Carol Lister. Doing a run on her name, I got a couple of pings on her credit card being used. She's not very bright.

The chick's not even trying to hide her footprints. It's like she wants to get caught. Or has no idea what she's doing. Anyway, she's holed up in a motel on San Remo Drive. I'll text you the address."

Bird gripped the back of the chair to stop himself from collapsing to the ground. His wife had been found. And she wasn't far away. He asked the question that had been burning through him from the second the news Imogene had been located. "Were you able to get eyes on Imogene?"

"Sorry, no. After she registered at the motel, she pulled her car around to one of the back units where the cameras aren't working."

"Fuck." That was the last thing Bird wanted to hear. He wanted Cass to say she'd seen Immy walking from the car. That she wasn't harmed.

"I'm sorry, but having no cameras working is to your advantage. The lighting is also shit," Cass continued. "I'll keep an eye on the cameras that are working and, if there's any movement between now and when you get to the location, I'll be able to let you know."

"Thanks, Cass, for everything," Fort said and disconnected the call. "Right, let's plan. We'll need to call the police and act as backup, but you know how they are. They work with us on situations like this."

"Don't worry, Bird. We'll get your woman," Silver said, a hard glint entering his eyes. The man was getting into the zone and Bird was grateful that he wasn't doing this alone.

* * *

IMOGENE'S STOMACH GRUMBLED AGAIN. It had been hours since she'd eaten anything. Before they'd gotten to the motel, Carol had stopped at a sandwich place and bought Imogene her favorite, ham and cheese on rye bread. If she thought that would get into Imogene's good graces, she was dreaming.

At present, Carol was muttering in the corner about the trips they'd planned. According to her kidnapper, they were going to Belize first, and then trekking through Peru. Neither one of those places appealed to Imogene. Her idea of a vacation was a nice beach house with the people she loved—Leighton and Layla. At the thought of her daughter, her heart ached. All she wanted to do was hold her baby. Would she ever do that again? See her beautiful little smile. Or see the way her green eyes sparkled in mischief before she did something she knew she could get in trouble for doing. Trace the little indentation in her chin. When she'd been born and she'd seen the same indentation that had marked her husband's face, Imogene had cried. The nurses thought it was the emotion of seeing her brand new baby, and of course, it was. But it was also the reminder of the man who'd owned her heart from the very second she saw him in the grocery store.

No matter what, she'd fight to see both of them again. No way was some delusional woman going to rob her of her life with her family.

"Carol, can we go get something to eat? Please."

Carol continued her muttering, completely ignoring her. What would happen if she just walked out the door? Would she even notice? Was she so lost in her fantasy world that nothing made sense anymore?

A knock sounded on the door and, immediately, Carol's demeanor changed. Gone was the catatonic woman and, in her place, was someone alert to her surroundings. Imogene bit her lip to keep from gasping when she saw Carol reaching for the gun.

The knock sounded again. "Pizza delivery."

"I didn't call for a pizza," Carol yelled through the door. "You've got the wrong room."

Call it instinct or hope, but Imogene believed with every fiber of her being that it wasn't a delivery man outside. She hoped she was right in thinking it was the police. What would be even better would be if it was Leighton.

Moving out of the direct line of the door, which was hard, considering the room was small, Imogene pressed herself into a corner, pulling the chair she'd been sitting on in front of her as a form of protection.

"The ticket says Carol Lister ordered a pizza. Can you just open the door? My boss is going fry my ass if I don't get back to the shop for another delivery." Whoever the person was, he'd injected the right amount of whine to his tone. Even Imogene believed what he said, even though she knew for a fact that Carol hadn't picked up the phone. Then again, Carol had been so lost in herself that maybe she would question if she had made the call and didn't remember.

Peering around the chair, Imogene saw that the look of lucidity had slipped from Carol's face again. Whatever was wrong with her definitely seemed serious.

"Open the door, Carol. I'm hungry. Don't you remember calling them? I do." Imogene crossed her fingers that Carol wouldn't dispute what she'd said.

"Ma'am, please, just open the door," the guy said as he knocked again. "The pizza's paid for and it's getting cold."

A shadow passed by the window and Imogene could make out the thin line of what looked like a rifle, causing her to slide down the wall behind her. The urge to leap up and run for the door was one she almost couldn't knock down. Only the thought that maybe they'd mistake her for Carol and start shooting kept her butt firmly on the floor.

Finally, after another knock, Carol opened the door. "I'm telling you—*oof.*" Two policemen rushed her and had her on the ground so fast Imogene almost didn't believe it was happening.

"Immy?"

Leighton? It couldn't be him. He was away on a mission. But there he was, striding through the room like an avenging angel. She stood and, the second she did, she was in his arms before she could even say his name.

"Oh, thank God, you're all right, Immy." He peppered her faces with kisses. "I love you. And I was so scared that something had happened to you and I wouldn't be able to hold you ever again."

His words tumbled out so fast, she couldn't comprehend them all. Her mind was still reeling with the fact that he was actually there holding her.

"Leighton, I love you too." She wasn't able to ask when he'd gotten back because his mouth clamped over hers in a crushing kiss. She wrapped her arms around him and the tears she'd been holding at bay from the second Carol forced her into the car, spilled over and ran down her cheeks.

Leighton pulled away and brushed his thumbs over

her cheeks. "You're okay, Immy. I've got you. I'll always have you. I will *always* find you."

"Bird, the cops need to speak to Imogene."

Imogene looked up and vaguely recognized the face of one of Leighton's team members. She thought it was the guy they called *Fort*. She really needed to get to know his team better than she had in the past.

"Fort, right?" The other man nodded. "Thank you."

"You're part of our team too. We will always have your back." His words were clipped, but there was a warmth to them, and she could tell he meant every single one of them.

"Do the cops really have to talk to her now?" Bird asked. "She's been through enough."

"It's okay, babe. I need to do this." In the background, she could hear Carol yelling obscenities as she was hand-cuffed and dragged to her feet. She pulled away from Leighton, needing to go over to the woman who'd kidnapped her. "Please wait," she said to the police.

They paused and looked at her, seeming surprised that she wanted to have anything to do with the other woman. When she was close enough, she met Carol's eyes. "I don't know why you did what you did, but you need help, Carol. You took me from my daughter and husband. I can't ever forgive you for doing that." She transferred her attention back to the police holding Carol. "Thanks."

As the officers escorted Carol out the door, Leighton's arm came around her waist and she leaned into him. He pressed a kiss to the top of her head. "I've got you. I love you."

She turned in his arms and rose up on her toes. "I know. I love you too." Pressing her lips against his, she poured all her love into the kiss and received the same in return.

She would forever be grateful that she'd gone to a picnic in San Antonio and found the love of her life...again.

EPILOGUE

THE DOORBELL RANG AND IMOGENE DROPPED THE GLASS she'd been holding. Leighton swooped in and caught it before it crashed to the ground.

"Are you sure you want to do this?" he asked. "It's only been a couple of weeks since you were taken."

She placed her hands over his. "Yes. I need to say thank you to everyone who helped you find me. Besides I want to get to know your teammates better. It's important to me."

"Okay, but if it gets to be too much, you tell me and I'll kick them all out."

Imogene pressed her lips against his. "I love you for that, but I'll be fine. It's a pity Parker couldn't make it. It would've been nice to see him again."

Leighton brushed his fingers over her wedding rings, an action he did on a regular basis. "Yeah, he seemed distracted and said there's some stuff going on. Not sure if it's work related or something else. He didn't go into too much detail. I'll phone him later tonight, or tomorrow and find out what's going on."

The doorbell buzzed again and this time the person who rang it didn't let up. "I think you need to let them in."

"Yeah, I do."

She admired the way Leighton's ass filled out his jeans as he walked out of the kitchen and headed toward the front door.

He'd been by her side the whole time she'd relayed her kidnapping to the police. Then she'd had to have a medical checkup, even though she'd insisted that Carol hadn't hurt her. The police had contacted her a week ago to tell her that Carol had been ordered to undergo a psych evaluation and also had charges pending in Texas for an assault against Trixie. The fact she hadn't laid a finger on Imogene was amazing. Then again, who knew what would've happened if Leighton and his team hadn't found her.

Determinedly, she pushed the thoughts aside. She had a party to get ready for.

The door opened and the noise level rose as Leighton's team traipsed into the house, closely followed by Ace and Piper their kids, and the rest of Ace's team. Layla squealed with delight at seeing her friends.

Two hours later, Imogene pushed items out of the way in the refrigerator looking for the cream she was sure she'd bought.

"Dammit, where is it?"

"Problem?" She glanced over shoulder and spied Fort standing behind her.

"Yeah, I thought I had some cream for the pie, but I can't find it."

159

"I'll run down to the convenience store and pick some up," Fort offered with a smile.

"Would you mind? I'd get Leighton to go, but he's putting Layla down for a nap." She still wasn't sure about Bird's team lead, but he was offering to help and she would take it.

"Not a problem. I'll be right back."

"Thanks."

Fort lifted a hand before he disappeared out the front door.

"Where's Fort going?" Leighton asked as he wandered back into the kitchen. He came up behind her and slid his arms around her waist, nuzzling her neck. Desire sizzled through her veins and she wanted to go outside and tell everyone to leave.

What had Leighton asked? Oh, right, Fort. "He's gone to get some cream for the pie."

"Cream, huh? I'll have to make sure I keep some aside for later on." He nipped her ear. "I can think of some really good things to do with it."

She laughed. "I can't wait to see. Love you, babe."

"Love you too." Forgetting about the friends in their backyard, they wrapped their arms around each other and gave themselves over the love that had strengthened until it was an unbreakable bond.

* * *

Knox 'Fort' Porter walked into the convenience store and scanned the area. There were only a handful of people in the store. He headed for the refrigerated section and spied a woman, her dark-blond hair caught up in a high ponytail. Her neck was slender, lending her the graceful look of a ballerina. He reached the section which held the cream and studied it. What sort did Imogene want? The one you whipped up by hand or the one that came out of a pressurized can.

Getting one of each seemed the best idea, that way he'd have both bases covered. He went to grab for the door at the same time as the woman he'd noticed earlier. Their hands touched and shaft of electricity sizzled from the connection up his arm, wrapping itself around him like a clinging vine.

"Oh, sorry. You go," she said and waved her hand toward the door. Her smile, open and friendly, slammed into him like a well-aimed punch to the gut.

"No, it's okay, you were here first."

She shrugged and pulled out a carton of half-and-half. "Thanks. Have a good day."

"You too," he muttered as she sauntered away, her hips swaying and the skirt of the green sundress she wore swishing in time. He shook his head to disperse the unusual reaction he was having to a complete stranger.

He reached into the fridge and picked up what he needed, letting the door slam shut. Screams rent the air and he immediately crouched behind a display of various soda boxes. Lifting his head slowly, he scanned the area, his blood turning to ice when he spied a man holding a gun against the side of the woman who'd been standing next to him.

"Fuck."

* * *

IF YOU ENJOYED this book please consider leaving a review. All reviews are greatly appreciated.

JOIN my Newsletter and find out about sales, free books, contests and new releases before anyone else! Click HERE

YOU CAN ALSO JOIN my reader group Nicole's Ninjas HERE

PARTIAL to sexy Alpha Navy Seals? If so, Protecting Lily is perfect for you. It's the first book in my Guardian Seals series and you can pick up a copy HERE.

DID YOU KNOW SAMANTHA, Rayne's sister from Rescuing Rayne has her own story? Pick up Rescuing Samantha HERE.

TO FIND out about new releases and sales follow me on Bookbub. Follow me.

ACKNOWLEDGMENTS

To the fantastic readers of the Special Forces Operation Alpha world - a huge Thank You for taking a chance on me and picking up my books. You are all awesome.

Susan and Amy, I'm honored to be part of the Aces Press family. This world grows and yet you both remain calm and so approachable.

To my fabulous Ninjas for always being there and supporting me, saying thank you never seems enough. Just know I appreciate and value every single one of you.

Huge shout out my wonderful cover artist and PA Jennifer. Once again you've created the perfect cover for this book.

Abigail, my writing partner, bestie and beta reader, you're an integral part of #TeamNicole. I count the day we met a huge blessing.

To Kay, thank you for running your eagle eye over my book and making it better.

Finally, my family who encourage and stand by me every day I'm working fills my heart with joy. Thank you for your unconditional love.

Falling for the Texan

A Merry Texan Christmas

Lovers Unmasked Series

Masquerade

Rescuing Dawn

Seducing Phoebe

Sweet Texas Secrets

Sweet Texas Fire

Man's Best Friend

Blind Date Bet

Next Door Knight

The Matchmaker's Match

The Elite

Fighting to Win

Fighting to Dream

Fighting for Love

Fighting for Redemption

The Freemasons

The Victor

The Hunter

Bound Series

Bound by Her Ring

Bound by His Desire

Bound by Their Love

Bound by The Billionaire's Desire - Boxed Set

Emerald Springs Legacy Series

Daniel's Decision

Emerald Springs Legacy Collection

Barefoot Bay

Swipe for Mr. Right

Wrong Time for Mr. Right

Novellas

Fighting Their Attraction

Tangled Vines

Tango Love

A Vacation Affair

Christmas in Ghost Gum Valley

Trapped by Cupid

Other Books in Sweet Texas Secrets Series

Sweet Texas Kiss by Monica Tillery

Sweet Texas Charm by Robyn Neeley

Other Books in Tarpley VFD Series

Fighting for Elena by Silver James

Fighting for Carly by Deanndra Hall

Fighting for Calliope by Haven Rose

Fighting for Jemma by MJ Nightingale

Fighting for Brittney by TL Reeve

ABOUT THE AUTHOR

On her very first school report her teacher said 'Nicole likes to tell her own stories'. Many years later she eventually sat down and wrote her first book.

Nicole writes sexy contemporary romances, seducing you one kiss at a time as you turn the pages. She enjoys taking two characters and creating unique situations for them.

When she's not writing, she's busy spreading glitter over social media and having a ton of fun doing it.

Learn more about Nicole Flockton at http://www. nicoleflockton.com. authornicole@nicoleflockton.com

Follow on:

Facebook: https://www. facebook.com/NicoleFlockton

Twitter: https://www.twitter.com/NicoleFlockton

Instagram: https://www. instagram.com/nicoleflockton

Goodreads: https://www.goodreads.com/author/ show/6479388.Nicole_Flockton

There are many more books in this fan fiction world than listed here, for an up-to-date list go to www.AcesPress.com

You can also visit our Amazon page at:
http://www.amazon.com/author/operationalpha

Special Forces: Operation Alpha World

KL Donn: Unraveling Love
Riley Edwards: Protecting Olivia
PJ Fiala: Defending Sophie
Nicole Flockton: Protecting Maria
Michele Gwynn: Rescuing Emma
Casey Hagen: Shielding Nebraska
Desiree Holt: Protecting Maddie
Kathy Ivan: Saving Sarah
Kris Jacen, Be With Me
Jesse Jacobson: Protecting Honor
Silver James: Rescue Moon
Becca Jameson: Saving Sofia
Kate Kinsley: Protecting Ava
Heather Long: Securing Arizona
Gennita Low: No Protection
Kirsten Lynn: Joining Forces for Jesse
Margaret Madigan: Bang for the Buck
Kimberly McGath: The Predecessor
Rachel McNeely: The SEAL's Surprise Baby
KD Michaels: Saving Laura
Lynn Michaels, Rescuing Kyle
Wren Michaels: The Fox & The Hound
Kat Mizera: Protecting Bobbi
Keira Montclair, Wolf and the Wild Scots
Mary B Moore: Force Protection
LeTeisha Newton: Protecting Butterfly
Angela Nicole: Protecting the Donna
MJ Nightingale: Protecting Beauty
Sarah O'Rourke: Saving Liberty
Victoria Paige: Reclaiming Izabel
Anne L. Parks: Mason
Debra Parmley: Protecting Pippa

Lainey Reese: Protecting New York
KeKe Renée: Protecting Bria
TL Reeve and Michele Ryan: Extracting Mateo
Elena M. Reyes: Keeping Ava
Angela Rush: Charlotte
Rose Smith: Saving Satin
Jenika Snow: Protecting Lily
Lynne St. James: SEAL's Spitfire
Dee Stewart: Conner
Harley Stone: Rescuing Mercy
Jen Talty: Burning Desire
Reina Torres, Rescuing Hi'ilani
Savvi V: Loving Lex
Megan Vernon: Protecting Us
Rachel Young: Because of Marissa

Delta Team Three Series
Lori Ryan: Nori's Delta
Becca Jameson: Destiny's Delta
Lynne St James, Gwen's Delta
Elle James: Ivy's Delta
Riley Edwards: Hope's Delta

Police and Fire: Operation Alpha World
Freya Barker: Burning for Autumn
B.P. Beth: Scott
Jane Blythe: Salvaging Marigold
Julia Bright, Justice for Amber
Anna Brooks, Guarding Georgia
KaLyn Cooper: Justice for Gwen
Aspen Drake: Sheltering Emma
Alexa Gregory: Backdraft

Deanndra Hall: Shelter for Sharla
Barb Han: Kace
EM Hayes: Gambling for Ashleigh
CM Steele: Guarding Hope
Reina Torres: Justice for Sloane
Aubree Valentine, Justice for Danielle
Maddie Wade: Finding English
Stacey Wilk: Stage Fright
Laine Vess: Justice for Lauren

Tarpley VFD Series
Silver James, Fighting for Elena
Deanndra Hall, Fighting for Carly
Haven Rose, Fighting for Calliope
MJ Nightingale, Fighting for Jemma
TL Reeve, Fighting for Brittney
Nicole Flockton, Fighting for Nadia

As you know, this book included at least one character from Susan Stoker's books. To check out more, see below.

SEAL of Protection: Legacy Series

Securing Caite

Securing Brenae (novella)

Securing Sidney

Securing Piper

Securing Zoey

Securing Avery

Securing Kalee

Securing Jane (Feb 2021)

SEAL Team Hawaii Series

Finding Elodie (Apr 2021)

Finding Lexie (Aug 2021)

Finding Kenna (Oct 2021)

Finding Monica (TBA)

Finding Carly (TBA)

Finding Ashlyn (TBA)

Delta Team Two Series

Shielding Gillian

Shielding Kinley

Shielding Aspen

Shielding Jayme (Jan 2021)

Shielding Riley (Jan 2021)

Shielding Devyn (May 2021)

Shielding Ember (Sept 2021)

Shielding Sierra (TBA)

Delta Force Heroes Series

Rescuing Rayne (FREE!)
Rescuing Aimee (novella)
Rescuing Emily
Rescuing Harley
Marrying Emily (novella)
Rescuing Kassie
Rescuing Bryn
Rescuing Casey
Rescuing Sadie (novella)
Rescuing Wendy
Rescuing Mary
Rescuing Macie (Novella)

Badge of Honor: Texas Heroes Series

Justice for Mackenzie (FREE!)
Justice for Mickie
Justice for Corrie
Justice for Laine (novella)
Shelter for Elizabeth
Justice for Boone
Shelter for Adeline
Shelter for Sophie
Justice for Erin
Justice for Milena
Shelter for Blythe
Justice for Hope
Shelter for Quinn
Shelter for Koren
Shelter for Penelope

SEAL of Protection Series

Protecting Caroline (FREE!)
Protecting Alabama
Protecting Fiona
Marrying Caroline (novella)
Protecting Summer
Protecting Cheyenne
Protecting Jessyka
Protecting Julie (novella)
Protecting Melody
Protecting the Future
Protecting Kiera (novella)
Protecting Alabama's Kids (novella)
Protecting Dakota

New York Times, USA Today and *Wall Street Journal* Bestselling Author Susan Stoker has a heart as big as the state of Tennessee where she lives, but this all American girl has also spent the last fourteen years living in Missouri, California, Colorado, Indiana, and Texas. She's married to a retired Army man who now gets to follow *her* around the country.

www.stokeraces.com
www.AcesPress.com
susan@stokeraces.com